He shouldn't touch her.

He was pushing the limits, testing his already strained self-control. For hours he'd been watching her smile and talk, worry and frown. He'd memorized the provocative way her lips quirked and her forehead creased, how her hair shimmered over her back. And all night long he'd been holding her, inhaling her feminine scent as he played the part of her fiancé.

It had been four hours of exquisite torture.

And if he didn't get away from her now, he was going to break. "It's late. You'd better go inside."

"I know." Her voice came out breathless. She stayed rooted in place.

He shifted closer, drawn to the heat in her eyes, the lure of her lush, sultry lips. He stroked his hands up her arms, his blood pumping hard. Hunger built in his veins.

To hell with self-control.

Dear Reader,

Who can resist the glitz and glamour of Las Vegas? Amanda Patterson certainly can! A down-on-her-luck single mother, Amanda moves to Sin City with one goal: provide her daughter with a safe and quiet life.

Unfortunately, Amanda's attempt to turn her luck around goes awry when she lands in the wrong place at the wrong time. Pursued by a killer and desperate to protect her young daughter, she moves in with billionaire casino mogul Luke Montgomery, who needs her to pose as his fiancée. Thrust into the ritzy world of the ultra-rich, Amanda feels like a modern-day Cinderella (albeit with a killer on her tail). But can this cynical, jaded billionaire bent on revenge really be her Prince Charming—or is trusting him a dangerous mistake?

I had a great time writing this book, and especially enjoyed working with the other authors in the series as we coordinated our tales. It was truly an honor to work with such a respected and talented bunch!

I hope you enjoy Luke and Amanda's journey—and that your own fairy tale comes true!

Gail Barrett

GAIL BARRETT

His 7-Day Fiancée

Silhouette®
Romantic
SUSPENSE

With thanks to Gail Barrett for her contribution to the
Love in 60 Seconds miniseries.

 SILHOUETTE BOOKS

Recycling programs
for this product may
not exist in your area.

ISBN-13: 978-0-373-27630-1
ISBN-10:   0-373-27630-3

HIS 7-DAY FIANCÉE

Visit Silhouette Books at www.eHarlequin.com

Printed in U.S.A.

GAIL BARRETT

always dreamed of becoming a writer. After living everywhere from Spain to the Bahamas, raising two children and teaching high school Spanish for years, she finally fulfilled that lifelong goal. Her writing has won numerous awards, including Romance Writers of America's prestigious Golden Heart. Gail currently lives in western Maryland with her two sons, a quirky Chinook dog and her own Montana rancher turned retired coast guard officer hero. Write to her at P.O. Box 65, Funkstown, Maryland 21734-0065, or visit her Web site, www.gailbarrett.com.

To my wonderful editor, Susan Litman, with appreciation for all that you've done. Thank you so much!

Acknowledgments

I'd like to thank the following people for their help: Destry Labo for answering my questions about Las Vegas; John K. Barrett, for his information about guns; Mary Jo Archer for her usual super help; and as always, Judith Sandbrook, critique partner extraordinaire. Thank you all!

Chapter 1

He was watching her again.

Fear razored through her belly like the slash of a switchblade—swift, hot, deep. It rippled through her awareness, stripped away her composure, shattering the illusion of safety she'd so desperately built.

Leaving her weak, defenseless, exposed.

No. Amanda Patterson wheezed air past her strangled throat, pressed her palm to her rioting heart. She wasn't weak, not anymore. And she refused to be vulnerable again.

She jerked her gaze past the line of stretch limos, inhaled deeply to steady her nerves. Cars idled by the casino on the gridlocked Strip, their horns blaring, stereos booming. Neon lights beckoned and flashed. And people streamed past, an endless parade of humanity—laughing, fearless people out to have fun on a warm April night.

She let out her breath, eased the death grip she had on her wrist, forced her shoulders to relax. She was imagining things. Wayne wasn't watching her. He wasn't even in Las Vegas. Her ex-husband was in Maryland, in prison, exactly where he belonged.

She was safe. *Safe.* She was thousands of miles away from Wayne, rid of him forever. She was in a new house, getting a new job, starting a new life.

Her sister, Kendall, finished paying the taxi driver and flashed her a smile. "Ready to rock?"

She dragged in another breath, tugged up the corners of her mouth. "You bet."

Kendall tilted her head. Her thick, honey-brown hair slid over her sculpted dancer's arms. "What's wrong? You're not worrying about Claire already are you?"

Her sister knew her too well. "No, of course not. Mrs. Schmidt seems great."

"She is great. And you warned her about Claire's allergies a dozen times. So stop worrying. Claire will have a great time. Mrs. Schmidt will spoil her to death."

To death. Amanda's heart squeezed. Dread shivered through her veins, but she shook off the gloomy thought. This was ridiculous. She was safe. Her three-year-old daughter was safe.

And she wasn't going to let her old fears ruin her new life.

"Then what is it?" Kendall probed. "It better not be Wayne because if you're going to let that creep—"

"It's not him. And I'm fine, really," she lied, embarrassed to let her sister know how rattled she was, how hard it was to quell that horrible feeling that he was spying on her, controlling her, even after all these months.

Kendall studied her with those perceptive hazel eyes.

Then her mouth softened. "Nothing's going to happen. You know that, right?"

"Right." She wouldn't let it. No matter how badly she'd mucked up the past, she owed her daughter a safe and stable life. Heck, she owed it to herself. She'd endured a hellish marriage, the terror of being stalked.

Now she was done with the past, done with the paranoia and fear—and on to a much better life.

She straightened her shoulders, tugged the hem of the tight red minidress Kendall had insisted she wear and tried for a lighter tone. "But getting arrested for indecent exposure isn't exactly what I need right now. Are you sure this dress is legal?"

Kendall tossed back her head and laughed, her trademark exuberance drawing the gazes of passing men. "Mandy, this is Vegas. The place where anything goes."

"Yes, I know, but—"

"But nothing. That dress is fabulous—although I still say you should have lost that ugly purse. Now, come on," she continued when Amanda opened her mouth to defend the huge, battered bag. "Lighten up. This is your lucky night out, remember?"

"Luck. Right." She latched on to Kendall's arm, turned toward the arched entrance to the famed Janus casino. "But walk slowly. I'm not used to these skyscraper heels."

"You're not used to having fun. Which is exactly why we're here. You're going to let loose for once— gamble, meet some hot men, have a ball."

Amanda grimaced. She had no intention of meeting men, hot or otherwise. She knew her limits too well. But Kendall was determined to light up the town, and the least she could do was try.

"Wait until you see this lobby," Kendall added as they

walked by a gleaming Bentley, then climbed the marble steps. "You're going to love it. It's right up your alley."

"My alley? Since when is gambling my thing?" She'd never placed a bet in her life.

"You'll see." The uniformed doorman swung the door open, and Kendall shot Amanda a knowing smile.

Amanda dutifully followed her inside. She gave herself a mental pep talk, tried to resist that constant urge to scan the crowds and monitor her surroundings for Wayne—a habit born of the need to survive. But she didn't need to worry about Wayne anymore. And she was *not* going to let him ruin this night.

She stepped past the doorway into the lobby, looked up and abruptly stopped. A huge, vaulted ceiling soared above her. Beneath it towered an enormous stone aqueduct, its tri-level arcades a marvel of ancient times.

"Oh, my," she murmured, and every thought of Wayne fled her mind. Captivated, she twirled in a circle, ignoring the people streaming around her, intent on absorbing every detail—the statues of Roman emperors, the decorative medallions and columns, the chariot perched on a marble dais.

"I told you," Kendall said while Amanda still gaped, trying to take it all in.

"You were right." This place was amazing. Fabulous. She felt as if she'd been dropped into ancient Rome.

Her gaze lingered on the colorful murals, the display of early black-glazed pottery, and the closet archaeologist in her thrilled. Whoever designed this place deserved an award. She couldn't believe how authentic it looked.

A woman brushed past, jostling her, and Amanda staggered to stay on her feet. She knew that she needed to move, that she was blocking the entrance, but she couldn't seem to budge. She wanted to absorb everything—the gurgling fountains, the flickering torches on the walls, the lions pacing restlessly behind glass. *Lions.* She shook her head, incredulous. This place was unreal.

Then her eyes settled on a plaster relief of Janus, and the tight ball knotting her belly began to slide loose. Janus, the Roman god of doorways and gates, endings and beginnings—the perfect symbol for her new life.

And for the first time in ages a sliver of optimism surged inside her, a long-buried glimmer of hope. She really was going to be all right here. She'd find a new job. Her daughter would thrive. She'd finally find the peace she deserved.

She smiled then, inhaling the soothing scent of moisture from the splashing fountains, the heavenly aroma of roses and gladioli brimming from urns. Still smiling, she turned to join her sister. The tang of a man's aftershave teased her nose.

Wayne's aftershave.

Her heart tripped. She stumbled, anxiety drumming through her. She glanced around, frantic to find the source of the scent, but a crowd formed around her, blocking her view.

Calm. Stay calm, she urged herself sternly. Wayne wasn't here. This had nothing to do with him.

She hauled in air, struggled to swallow around the tension gripping her throat, determined not to overreact. She stepped to the side, tried to work her way through the noisy throng to find where her sister had gone. But the people shifted and trapped her in.

"Get out of my way," a man in a white shirt shouted beside her, and his rough, raised voice agitated her nerves.

"The hell I will," another man answered.

Amanda glanced up, caught the first man's glowering face and took another step back. They were too close. Too close. Trying to beat back the onrush of panic, she cleared her throat. "Excuse me."

They ignored her. Her anxiety building, she prodded the nearest man with her elbow, intent on getting past. But another whiff of aftershave curled through her senses, and her heart made a frenzied throb.

Stop it, she lectured herself. She had no reason to be afraid. This man had nothing to do with Wayne.

And these people were not going to hurt her. She had to get over the irrational fear, this wrenching need to escape.

She pivoted, wobbled on her too-high heels, determined to get free of this mess. But then a fistfight broke out. Someone shoved. The white-shirted man pushed back, sending the beefy man into her side. Thrown off balance, she gasped, dropped her purse, and nearly fell. The contents of her handbag spilled over the floor.

Great.

Her hands trembling, urgency making her head light, she knelt, scooped up her cell phone and keys. The man in the white shirt squatted beside her. "Sorry," he muttered, his voice gruff. His aftershave assailed her, setting off a spurt of panic, unleashing a bone-deep reaction she couldn't control.

"Just leave it. Please. It doesn't matter," she pleaded, needing him to move far away. But he snatched up her wallet and tissues with his thick, stubby fingers, and stuffed them into her bag. Desperate now, unable to meet his eyes, she grabbed her purse, clutched it to her chest and rose.

"Break it up!" someone shouted as she turned and stumbled away from the arguing men. She searched through the crowd for her sister, found her waiting a few yards away.

"There you are," her sister said. "What are you doing?"

"Nothing." Her voice came out high and rushed, and she sucked in a calming breath. "I just got bumped and my purse spilled."

"I told you not to bring that bag."

"I know." She reopened the drawstring top, pawed through the jumbled contents, double-checked that her wallet was there. Relief flooded through her, and she blew out her pent-up breath.

"Well, try to keep up this time," Kendall said, and shook her head.

Feeling foolish, berating her loss of control, she trailed her sister across the room. So she'd smelled Wayne's aftershave. Big deal. He'd worn a popular brand. She'd let her imagination run away from her.

And she had to stop it. She couldn't keep letting him do this to her. Every time she thought of him, he won.

But as they crossed the enormous lobby—past the restless lions, past the Roman arches leading to intriguing gardens and baths—that feeling of trepidation crept through her again, as if eyes were boring into her back. She straightened her shoulders, determined not to assume that submissive hunch, and tried to shrug the sensation off. But it only intensified, crawling up her spine, her neck, growing stronger with every step.

Her temper flared. This was ridiculous. She didn't deserve this constant fear. She had to put an end to the lunacy now.

"Wait a minute," she said to Kendall. Defiant, she stopped, whipped around.

And met the dark, searing eyes of a man.

But not the one who'd bumped her. This man stood apart from the rest, his feet planted wide, his hands braced low on his hips, like an ancient conqueror surveying his realm.

His thick black hair gleamed in the lights. Heavy beard stubble shadowed his jaw. He had black, slashing brows, taut, masculine cheeks and a mouth so sensual it made her breath catch. A black suit gloved his tall frame.

He was handsome, riveting—shockingly so. But more than his dark looks commanded attention. He had a stillness about him, a feral intensity that exuded intelligence, authority, power.

Her heart thumped, made a funny zigzag in her chest. The word *predator* flashed through her mind.

The edge of his mouth kicked up at her blatant inspection. His eyes smoldered even more. Then his own gaze dropped, making a long, slow slide over the length of her, trailing a firestorm of heat in its wake.

Her knees trembled. A zap of awareness sizzled her blood. And a completely different type of tension arose in her nerves.

Her face burning, she whirled back toward her sister.

"Whoa, when I said hot men, I didn't mean that hot," Kendall said.

"What?" Breathless, mortified that she'd responded so outrageously, she grabbed her sister's arm and hauled her away.

"You know who that was, don't you? That was Luke Montgomery. *The* Luke Montgomery. Oh, for goodness sakes," Kendall said when she shot her a blank look.

"Don't you know anything? He's the billionaire who owns this place."

"You're kidding." She'd been ogling a billionaire? How ridiculous could she get?

"No, I'm not kidding. And I can't believe you haven't heard of him. He's been in the news for weeks. You know, because of that woman who was murdered, that casino heiress, Candace Rothchild?"

"No." Amanda slowed to navigate the steps into the gaming pit. She'd been too worried about her own precarious situation to follow the news.

Her sister paused at the bottom of the stairs and huffed out her breath. "You're hopeless. It's a good thing you're in my hands now. I'll get you caught up on tabloid gossip and have you living in sin in no time."

"Great." A wry smile nudged the corner of her mouth. "Just what I need. My own personal guide to corruption."

Kendall grinned back. "Hey, don't knock it."

"I'm not." Her sister might not lead a conventional life, but she did know how to have fun. And at least she hadn't screwed everything up like Amanda had.

Determined to forget all that, she glanced around at the flashing lights and jangling machines, the kaleidoscope of colors and noise. "All right, what's first?"

"Slots. Once you win a little, gain some confidence, we'll graduate to blackjack."

Amanda sighed. She was pathetic. Even her sister knew she couldn't just plunge in and enjoy herself. She had to be coaxed in slowly, teased into having fun.

Her sister took her arm, led her down the aisle to a couple of empty stools. "Here. These machines are loose. They pay out more often."

"How do you know that?"

Kendall propped one slim hip on the stool, squirmed to keep her own short dress from creeping up. "They do it on purpose. They figure if you win here, they can lure you back to the tables and steal your shirt. Now sit down and listen up."

Amanda slid onto the next stool over. She placed her purse on her lap, her amusement growing as her sister gave her a crash course on gambling with slots.

Not that her sister's expertise surprised her. Growing up, Kendall had been everything Amanda was not—confident, popular, outgoing. She'd been the star of every party, the diva on every stage. And she hadn't been afraid to pursue her goals. The day after high school ended she'd hopped on the first bus to Vegas and landed her dream job dancing in a show.

Whereas the far-too-cautious, ever-responsible Amanda had become a teacher and married Wayne.

"Got it?" Kendall asked.

Amanda pulled her thoughts from the past. "I think so." She tugged a twenty dollar bill from her wallet and fed it into the machine, saw the credits appear.

"Here goes." She inhaled, selected the maximum number of coins, and pushed the button to spin the machine. Bars whirred, then stopped. More credits appeared, and she widened her eyes. "Hey, I won."

"I knew you would." Kendall's smile was smug. "I told you your luck was going to change tonight."

"Maybe so." Buoyed by that small success, she pushed the button again. Three lemons. Getting the hang of it now, she threw herself into the game. Cherries combined with sevens. Lemons were followed by bars. Bells dinged. Colored lights flashed. Credits accumulated, then disappeared. Beside her, Kendall cheered, groaned and clapped at her own progress. And a half hour and a free margarita later, Amanda felt like a seasoned pro.

"Ready for the blackjack table?" Kendall called over the noise.

Amanda glanced up. "Go ahead. I'll be there in a minute. I've just got a few pulls left."

"Okay. It's in the back." Kendall drained her drink, hopped off her stool and then jiggled her legs to straighten her dress. "Don't forget to take your ticket. We'll cash out before we leave."

Amanda waved her off and returned her attention to her machine. In the periphery of her vision, she saw Kendall collect her ticket and leave.

She pulled the lever. Lemon-bar-seven. *Drats.* She pushed the button again and won. She grinned, pleased with her take so far. Not too shabby for her first attempt at gambling. She was ahead by fifteen bucks.

And she had to hand it to her sister. It was fun to do something mindless for once, to forget her problems and relax. Kendall had been right to insist that they come.

She gave the button a final press, then waited for the tumbler to stop. "Come on, jackpot," she murmured. A seven stuck. Then another. She held her breath, her hopes rising, her eyes glued on the machine.

The scent of Wayne's aftershave drifted past.

Her heart went still. Every cell in her body tensed.

The machine stopped. She stared at it blindly, her palms suddenly sweating, her pulse pounding so hard she could barely hear.

Wayne wasn't here. He couldn't be here.

Then why was this happening to her?

She gripped her purse like a lifeline, fought the urge to glance over her shoulder and check. She couldn't keep doing this. She couldn't keep panicking and falling apart. Dear God, it had to stop.

But the need to look back grew even stronger—the instinct to protect herself, take cover. *Survive.* Unable to stand it, she leaped from the stool and whipped around.

No one was there.

She didn't move.

Lights flashed on another machine. A woman squealed and laughed down the aisle. Amanda hitched out her breath, ran her gaze up and down the rows, but there was no sign of the man who'd bumped her, no sign of Wayne.

Thoroughly rattled, she turned back to her machine and printed out her credits with trembling hands. Had she imagined that scent? Was that even possible? Her mentally ill mother had hallucinated before she'd—

No. She was not losing her mind.

Maybe it was a flashback, a delayed reaction to stress. The past few years had worn her down completely—Wayne's abuse, the constant fear for her daughter's safety, the painful divorce and move. No wonder she was suffering now.

And she would conquer this fear. *She would.*

Her heart still racing, she inhaled to calm her nerves. Then she walked deliberately toward the back of the casino, refusing to let herself rush. There was nothing to be afraid of. Nothing.

She paused at the end of the aisle, unsure which way to go. Taking a guess, she turned right.

The scent of aftershave hit her again.

Her stomach balled tight. Her heart sped into her

throat. She picked up the pace, walking faster now, even though she knew there was nothing wrong. She was safe, *safe*.

She hurried past a group of noisy gamblers. A bell dinged, and someone cheered. Knowing she was acting foolish but unable to stifle the fear, she walked as fast as she could on the spindly heels. *Run, run, run* bludgeoned her nerves.

She reached the end of the aisle, turned again, then reached some swinging doors. Oh, no. She'd gone the wrong way. The blackjack tables had to be across the pit.

She stopped, started to turn, but Wayne's scent swarmed her again. A hard, narrow object bit into her back, and she froze.

"That's right," the man said. "Stay quiet, and you won't get hurt."

Her knees buckled. A dull roar invaded her skull. The obscene smell of aftershave permeated the air.

"Walk over to the doors. Slow now." He rammed the gun deeper into her back, and she stepped forward, trying to battle through the hysteria and think. It wasn't Wayne. He had the wrong voice. But then what on earth did he want?

"Stop," he demanded when she reached the double doors. "Now give me the ring. And no fast moves."

"R…ring?" He wanted her jewelry? But she didn't wear any. She wheezed in the too-thick air. "But—"

"Now." His voice turned harsher. He prodded her again with the gun.

"But I don't…"

The double doors swung open. A waitress stepped out, balancing a tray.

Now or never.

She lunged, slammed into the waitress. The woman shrieked, staggered back and dropped the tray.

Amanda didn't hesitate. She ran.

Chapter 2

The soft buzz of his private telephone line cut through the silence—muted, deceptively quiet, like the rattle of a Mojave Desert Sidewinder preparing to strike. Luke Montgomery stared out his penthouse window at the Las Vegas skyline shimmering against the dark velvet sky. He'd left instructions not to be disturbed. A call now could only mean one thing.

Trouble. Just what he didn't need.

He exhaled, knowing he couldn't postpone the inevitable, and padded across the carpet to his desk. He punched the button to answer the phone. "Yeah."

"Mr. Montgomery. Frank Ruiz in security. I'm sorry to bother you, but there was an armed robbery attempt in the gaming pit. I thought you'd want to know."

"I'll be right there."

Luke disconnected the phone and frowned. An armed robbery attempt. Interesting timing with the investment consortium scheduled to vote in just two weeks. A coincidence or something more?

Thoughtful, he pulled his suit jacket from the chair where he'd tossed it, slipped it on as he strode to the door. Coincidence or not, he couldn't afford the bad publicity. Candace Rothchild's murder had caused enough problems.

Not that being suspected of murder had hurt his business. He exited his penthouse, the edge of his mouth ticked up in a cynical smile. Crowds flocked to his casino, whipped up by lurid rumors in the tabloids, hoping to glimpse the man who'd supposedly clubbed the heiress to death.

But his consortium investors weren't nearly as intrigued. The murder—combined with the downturn in the economy—had made them nervous. Too nervous. More problems now would cause them to bolt.

And no way could he let that happen.

His gaze hardening, he crossed to his private elevator, then leaned back against the mahogany panels as it started down. He had everything riding on this project. He'd spent twenty years meticulously constructing his empire, amassing money, power.

Twenty years plotting revenge.

The elevator doors slid open, and he headed toward the security office, ignoring the employees scurrying out of his way. Nothing could jeopardize this project. Nothing. If this robbery attempt was legit, he'd hush it up, keep it out of the papers until the deal went through. And if it wasn't…

He mentally shrugged. Whoever had planned this escapade had made a mistake, a big one. No one played Luke Montgomery for a fool.

A lesson the Rothchilds should have learned long ago.

He entered the office, met the eyes of the guard on duty behind the desk. The balding man leaped to his feet. "Mr. Montgomery." He tugged at the tie dangling from his beefy neck.

Luke nodded, got straight to the point. "What's going on?"

"A woman said she was held up at gunpoint near the slot machines. I've pulled up the surveillance tapes. She's in the next room."

"Let's see the tapes." He rounded the desk as Ruiz lowered himself into his chair and keyed the bank of monitors to the proper time.

The screens flickered, and suddenly a woman strolled into view from a dozen angles. Her full hips swiveled with a seductive swing. Her high breasts shifted and swayed.

Luke's gaze cut to her face, and his heart made a sudden swerve. Well, hell. It was the blonde he'd admired earlier in the lobby.

He studied her now with frank appreciation. She was on the tall side, slender, but the tight dress revealed her ample curves. She had long, shiny hair, sweetly rounded hips, the kind of killer legs that could fuel his fantasies for years.

He slanted his head. She wasn't the usual overblown Vegas type, despite the skimpy dress. She seemed more natural, unstudied—a rarity in Sin City, a place where illusions ruled.

She stumbled on the mile-high heels, regained her balance and glanced around. The cameras caught her darting gaze, and his gut went still.

She looked furtive. Guilty.

Bad move, babe. Better to look nervous *after* the guy with the gun shows up.

As if on cue, a man appeared on scene. The newcomer kept his head bent low, his face carefully hidden from the camera's view. His long, stringy hair swung past his jaw, hiding his features even more.

Luke's gaze narrowed on the man's pleated blue shirt and black bow tie—the uniform his dealers wore. "Is he one of ours?"

"We don't know yet. We're checking the records now."

He rubbed his stubble-roughened jaw, watched the episode play out. The galley doors swung open. A waitress stepped out, carrying a tray. The blonde crashed into her, then bolted off, while the man ran the other way.

He raised a brow. The blonde thought fast on her feet, he'd give her that much. "Who is she?"

The guard consulted his notes. "Amanda Patterson. Said she arrived in Las Vegas last week. She's staying with her sister, Kendall Patterson, a dancer in your ten-o'clock show."

Luke thought back to the brunette he'd seen with her in the lobby. A dealer and a dancer. An inside job, then? Probably a scam to sue the casino.

The spurt of disappointment took him by surprise. He knew better than to expect the blonde to be innocent. This was Vegas. Everyone was on the make. Even the prettiest face masked a conniving heart.

The guard switched to another screen, and Luke watched the man exit the casino, still hiding his face. He checked the time on the tape. Twenty minutes ago. No point looking for him now.

"Let me know what the employee search brings up. Contact legal, call the police. Get Martinez over here if you can." He and Martinez went way back to their childhood in Naked City, the slums beyond the Strip. He could count on him to keep the story hushed until the Phoenix deal went through.

He turned, headed down the hall to interview the blonde. Chances were that this was an inside job, but he couldn't rule out the Rothchilds. Harold Rothchild was buried in debt, his empire on the verge of collapse. Luke's project would seal his doom.

Which was exactly what Luke planned.

Of course, if the Phoenix project failed, he would suffer instead. He set his jaw. Good thing he didn't intend to fail.

He pushed open the office door, spotted the blonde standing by the desk. She turned toward him as he entered the room.

His gaze met hers. A sudden awareness shivered between them, and he hesitated in midstride.

She was even more attractive close up. Her eyes were a deep, startling blue, as vibrant as the desert sky. She had pale, creamy skin, a smattering of freckles on her feminine nose. Her lips looked soft and lush.

She was pretty, damned pretty—stunning if he factored in those world-class legs.

But this close he could also sense an aura of vulnerability about her. She stood with her shoulders hunched, her arms crossed tightly across her chest. Dark circles shadowed her eyes.

The sudden urge to protect her caught him off guard.

He frowned, shook himself out of his daze. This woman didn't need his protection. For all he knew, she was here to swindle him. "Amanda Patterson?"

"Yes." Her low, smoky voice slid through him, doing strange things to his insides.

He crossed the room. "I'm Luke Montgomery."

"Yes, I know, I…" A blush crept up her cheeks. "My sister pointed you out earlier."

He'd bet. He reached out his hand. She hesitated, then gripped his palm. The smooth, silky feel of her skin arrowed through him, deleting his thoughts. He was held immobile by those amazing blue eyes. His heart beat hard in his chest.

After several long moments, he realized he was still holding her hand. He scowled, pried his fingers loose, annoyed by the effort it took. What the hell was that about? He hadn't been that affected by a woman in years.

And this one could be trying to deceive him.

"Have a seat." Anxious to put some distance between them, he retreated to the desk, then leaned back against it and folded his arms.

She perched on the leather chair in front of the desk and crossed her legs. His gaze fell to her lean, bare thighs, traced the elegant curve of her calves. Realizing his thoughts were derailing again, he lifted his eyes.

"So what happened?" His tone was more brusque than he'd intended, and she blinked.

She sat up straighter, flexed her wrist as if it ached. Her chest rose as she drew in a breath. "I was going to the blackjack tables to find my sister, but I got lost. I've never been here before. I started to turn around but then a…a man came up behind me."

Her voice trembled convincingly, but he was determined to stay objective. "He was armed?"

"I think so. He jabbed something into my back. I thought…it felt like a gun."

"Then what?"

"He said…he wanted my jewelry, my ring."

His gaze cut to her unadorned ears, to the cleavage bared by the plunging dress, and his mind flashed back to the tapes. He hadn't noticed any jewelry before the attack. A slipup there.

"So you handed it over?" he asked, knowing damned well she hadn't.

But she surprised him by shaking her head. "No, I…I don't have any jewelry, not anymore." She lifted one slender shoulder and lowered her eyes. "I sold everything a while back when I needed the money."

So she was short on cash. Good motive to run a scam.

He pinched the bridge of his nose and sighed. No matter how attractive she was, he didn't have time for this farce. He'd make sure the Rothchilds weren't involved, keep this damned thing out of the news, then let the police handle the rest.

"So you're saying a man held you up with a gun you didn't see, and demanded jewelry that you don't have."

A small frown creased her brow. "You don't believe me? You think I made this up?"

"We have cameras all over the casino. I saw the tapes." He raised his brows. "You looked nervous even before the man showed up."

Her smooth lips parted. The color drained from her face. "But that's because I thought…I thought…" She pressed her fingers to her lips and closed her eyes.

"You thought what? That you'd pretend to be attacked and sue the casino?"

Her eyes flew open, and she gasped. "You think I'd pretend about something like that? Are you joking?"

She let out a high-pitched laugh. "Oh, God. This figures. I thought…" She shook her head, gathered her bulky purse and rose. "Forget it."

"The hell I will." He pushed himself away from the desk and blocked her path. "You thought what?"

"Nothing. It doesn't matter." She tried to step around him, but he reached out and grabbed her upper arm. She flinched, jerked back. "Let me go."

He dropped her arm, stunned by the urgency in her voice, the flash of fear in her eyes. She quickly scuttled away.

He studied her, taken aback. She couldn't be this good of an actress. She was actually afraid of him.

He eased apart his hands, made his expression neutral, his voice nonthreatening so she wouldn't bolt. "Look, I'm not trying to hurt you. I just need to know what happened."

"I…" She nodded, sucked in her breath, as if to pull herself together. "I didn't really… It was just…my ex-husband. Wayne Wheeler. I thought he was here."

He eyed the distance she'd put between them, the wary way she watched him—defensive, alert, like a cornered animal ready to run. And anger stirred in his gut. He had no patience for abusive men. And unless he was wildly off base, this woman had been attacked.

He struggled to keep the emotion from his voice. "Your ex lives around here?"

She shook her head, sending her silky hair sliding over her arms. "He's in Maryland, in jail. It wasn't him. It wasn't even his voice. But I thought, earlier… I was just nervous. I overreacted. I'm sorry." She rubbed her forehead with a trembling hand, sank back into her chair.

He frowned. He didn't doubt her story. Her fear looked real... And the facts would be easy to check.

So what should he do about it? Assuming she was telling the truth, this still didn't eliminate the Rothchilds' involvement. Or her sister's. It wouldn't be the first time an unsuspecting family member had been an accomplice to a crime.

Which led him back to his original problem. He paced across the room, pivoted, then returned to lean against the desk. He had to contain this, keep it out of the news. He couldn't let that consortium implode.

Which meant making sure Amanda Patterson didn't talk.

But somehow the thought that anyone would hurt this gentle woman made it hard to stay detached.

"I need to go." Her eyes pleaded with his. "My sister will be wondering where I am. I left her a voice mail that I'd meet her in the lobby."

"You can leave as soon as you talk to the police." A knock sounded on the door, and he rose. "That's probably the detective now. I'll walk you out to the lobby when you're done."

"All right." Their gazes held. The vulnerable look in her eyes tugged at something inside him, urging him to shelter her, to keep her safe.

He shook it off. Her life, her problems were none of his concern. The only thing he needed to do was convince her not to talk. But she had been attacked in his casino. He could at least alleviate some of her fear. He turned, strode out the door.

Ramón Martinez from the Las Vegas Metropolitan Police Department was waiting for him in the hall. "Martinez." Luke shook his hand, briefed him on the situation, and the need to keep it quiet for now. "Could you check on the ex and make sure he's still in jail?" he added. "The name's Wheeler. Wayne Wheeler."

"No problem." The detective flipped open his cell phone, called in the information. "It'll take a few minutes to run him through the system. I'll get a statement from the Patterson woman and get back to you on that."

"Thanks." Luke returned to the main office, had his security guard run the tapes again as he waited for the detective to finish up. Now that he'd heard Amanda's version of events, the anxiety in her eyes made sense.

His gaze lingered on the seductive flare of her hips, those endless legs. It was too bad she wasn't his type. She was a damned attractive woman. But he only dated celebrities, supermodels, women willing to hang on his arm for an evening in exchange for a fancy meal.

He didn't have relationships, and he didn't mix dating with business. And that's all Amanda Patterson could ever be—a business concern. One he needed to wrap up now.

She emerged from the office a few minutes later. "I heard back about Wheeler," Martinez said from behind her. "He's still in jail."

"Good." He caught Amanda's gaze, and that disturbing attraction rocked through him again. His eyes dipped from her face to those killer legs, and he had to struggle to remember his plan. "I'll walk you out."

He nodded to the detective, held the door open for Amanda, then accompanied her down the carpeted hall. He liked how her long strides kept pace with his, how her height made it easy to meet her eyes.

"Thanks for checking on Wayne for me," she said, her voice subdued. "It helps to know he's far away." Her eyes held his, and the worry lurking in those vivid eyes bothered him more than he cared to admit.

"No problem. I have a favor to ask, though." They reached the door to the lobby, and he paused. "I'd like to keep this incident out of the news—at least for a couple of weeks. I'm in the middle of some negotiations right now, and I don't want the publicity. So if anyone calls you—any reporters, the tabloids—I'd appreciate it if you didn't talk."

"Okay."

"The paparazzi can be persistent," he warned her. "I doubt they'll get wind of this, but if they do they'll call, show up at your door, follow you around."

"But that's ridiculous." Her forehead wrinkled. "Why would they care what happened to me?"

"They won't. But I'm big news these days."

"I see." She bit her lip, made that flexing motion with her wrist again.

He frowned. "Did you get hurt back there?"

"What?" She looked at her wrist. "Oh. No, it's an old injury. It aches sometimes."

He nodded, tugged his business card from his inside pocket and held it out, determined to make sure she complied. "Here's my number. Call me if they show up. I'll top whatever they're willing to pay."

She blinked, shot him a look of disbelief. "You're offering to pay me not to talk?"

"I told you that I don't want the publicity right now."

"Well, neither do I." Stunned outrage tinged her voice. "I have a daughter to protect. I don't want to be in the news."

But money had a way of changing minds. And the tabloids' pockets were deep. "Take the card, Amanda." He pressed it into her hand. "Just call me if they contact you."

She glanced at the card and shook her head. "There's really no need. I told you that I won't talk."

He let out a cynical laugh. "Promises don't mean much when money's involved."

"Well, mine does."

Her eyes simmered with indignation.

He tilted his head, impressed. Despite her air of fragility, the woman had courage. He liked how she held her ground.

Hell, he liked a lot of things about her. His gaze lowered, traced the sultry swell of her lips, then flicked back to her brilliant blue eyes. And hunger pulsed inside him, the slow, drugging beat of desire.

But this woman had no place in his plans. He stepped away, crushing back the urge to touch her, giving them some much-needed space.

She cleared her throat. "I'd say good-night, but it hasn't really been good, has it?"

"No, not good." Especially with this disturbing attraction between them.

"Farewell, then." She turned, pushed open the door.

He followed her into the lobby, then stopped, inhaling deeply to clear his mind. His eyes tracked the alluring swivel of her hips as she continued across the marble floor. She joined her sister, and the two women walked to the door.

But suddenly she paused, glanced back. Her eyes met his, and another bolt of electricity zapped his nerves. Then she pivoted on her high heels and went out the door.

For a long moment, he just stood there, the image of

those lush lips and long legs scorched in his brain. Then he slowly eased out his breath.

So that was done. She was gone. He had no reason to see her again. His security chief and the police could handle the investigation from here.

He hoped her ex-husband left her alone, though. He hated to think of her afraid, cowering before some brute.

And he hoped that he could trust her. Amanda Patterson was a wild card, an unknown, someone beyond his control.

Someone, he had a feeling, it would take a very long time to forget.

Chapter 3

The telephone was ringing again.

Amanda sat motionless on her sister's patio, her muscles tensing, the teaching application she'd filled out forgotten in her hand.

"Phone, Mommy," Claire announced from her turtle-shaped sandbox in the yard.

"I know." Amanda tried not to let fear seep into her voice. "But Aunt Kendall's at rehearsal. We'll let the answering machine pick it up." And hope to God it wasn't another hang-up call.

The answering machine kicked on, and her sister's perky voice floated through the open sliding glass door. The machine beeped. The abrupt silence of the disconnected line made her stomach churn.

She set down her papers and rubbed her arms—chilled now, despite the heat. It was just another wrong number or a junk phone call. There was nothing sinister about people calling and hanging up. Annoying, yes. Dangerous, no.

Even if the hang-up calls had only begun three days ago, after the casino attack. Even if they now got a dozen such calls a day. Even if whenever she answered the phone, there was only heavy, ominous breathing— nothing more.

It couldn't be reporters. They would talk to her, ask questions, not just breathe and hang up.

This was something Wayne would do—something he had done to unsettle her nerves. But Wayne was in jail. That detective had checked.

She set her pen on the table and rose, placed a rock over the job application so it wouldn't flutter away. Regardless of who was calling, she wasn't going to let this get to her. And she wasn't going to let Claire sense her fear. She'd moved here to give her daughter a safer, more peaceful life, and she would succeed.

"It's time to get the mail and have our snack." She struggled to make her voice cheerful, but Claire still looked at her and frowned. "How about some apple juice and animal crackers today?"

"Okay." Claire trotted over, and Amanda brushed the sand off her daughter's bottom and hands, adjusted the sun hat flopping around her sweet face.

"Wait. Brownie." Claire grabbed the bear she'd propped on the patio chair and hugged it close. Too close. Had Claire picked up on her fear?

She forced a smile to lighten the mood. "Is Brownie going to help us get the mail?" She knew the answer, of course. Claire didn't go anywhere without her bear. Brownie ate with her, slept with her, played with her.

She'd hugged off most of its fur, kissed the color from its once-black eyes. Amanda prayed that bear never got lost, or Claire would be destroyed.

"You two can lead the way," she added, and followed her along the walkway to the gate. Her sister lived in one of the new developments that had sprung up during the recent building boom. It was a modest, family-oriented neighborhood with two-story stucco homes, a far cry from Wayne's luxury condo at the Ritz Carlton in DC. And thank goodness for that. Wayne had been all about status, appearances. He didn't care that there'd been no place for Claire to ride a bike or play.

She unlatched the gate, waited for Claire to toddle through. She couldn't even begin to imagine how Luke Montgomery lived. She'd read up on him during the past few days, learned that he was a notorious playboy, a megabillionaire developer who owned casinos and resorts throughout the world. That suit he'd worn had probably cost more than her car.

An image of his broad, muscled shoulders, the dark, sexy planes of his face flashed into her mind. She didn't doubt the playboy part. The man was lethally attractive with his deeply graveled voice and intense eyes. And that moment in the hallway when she'd thought he was going to kiss her…

She shut the gate behind her with a forceful click. Surely she'd imagined his interest in her. Luke Montgomery operated completely outside her orbit—which was fine with her. She had all she wanted in life right here. Maybe she didn't hobnob with billionaires, and maybe she'd once dreamed of a more exciting life, but she had a great sister, a daughter she adored. And soon she'd have a job and her own house, too.

She just needed to lose this constant fear.

"Wait for me," she warned Claire. She grabbed her daughter's hand to make sure she didn't dart off, then walked with her toward the mailbox. The warm sun shimmered off the neighbors' red-tiled roofs. Palm fronds rustled in the breeze. Laughter and the thump of a bouncing basketball came from some teens shooting hoops down the street.

She let Claire open the mailbox and pull out the advertisements and bills. She lunged forward to catch a sheath of junk mail tumbling loose.

"Mine," Claire cried and clutched the mail.

"I'm just getting the stuff that fell." She scooped up the ads and stray letters and then closed the box. A plain white envelope in her hand caught her eye.

She paused, turned it over. No name. No address.

A sliver of foreboding snaked up her back.

She shook it off, exasperated by her overreaction. She was getting ridiculous, imagining danger at every turn. It was probably an advertisement. She tore open the back flap, pulled out the contents—a piece of white paper, some photos.

Photos of Claire.

Her heart stopped.

She flipped through the photos. Claire riding her pink tricycle. Claire eating at the kitchen table. Claire sleeping next to Brownie in her bed.

The air turned thick. Her hands shook as she unfolded the note. *"Put the diamond in the mailbox or else."*

Her lungs seized up. Sheer panic roared through her veins. She fought to maintain her composure, but every instinct screeched at her to snatch Claire up and flee.

Calm down, she ordered herself fiercely. Don't let Claire see your fear.

Forcing her feet to move slowly, normally, she followed her daughter back to the house. She looked casually to the neighbor's windows—no movement there. She opened the gate and let Claire through, then snuck a glance at the street. Empty.

But someone was spying on them, taking photos of Claire.

Her panic intensified, threatening to overwhelm her, but she ruthlessly crushed it down. She ushered Claire calmly into the house and locked the sliding glass door. She lifted Claire to the sink and washed her hands. Still working on autopilot, she took out the juice, helped Claire into her chair, opened the animal crackers and propped up the bear.

"What's wrong, Mommy?" Claire asked, her voice tight.

"Nothing. Nothing at all." Her falsely cheerful voice sounded too far away. "It's just a little hot in here. I'm going to close the drapes to keep it cool. I'll be right back."

She forced her lips into a brittle smile, closed the blinds on the sliding glass door and strolled sedately into the hall. Then she raced around the house like a maniac, locking the windows, yanking the drapes closed, scrambling up and down the stairs, rushing from room to room to room, throwing the deadbolts on every door.

She returned to the kitchen, sank into a seat across the table from Claire and covered her face with her hands. What on earth was going on here? What diamond? She'd sold her wedding ring as soon as she'd left Wayne.

Besides, Wayne was in jail. It couldn't be him.

Unless he'd hired someone else to harass her.

Trying to compose herself, she scrubbed her face with her quivering hands. God, she was sick of this. So bloody tired. All she wanted was a life without fear. Was that too much to ask?

The phone rang.

She jerked up her head, stared at the phone. Her palms started to sweat.

The ringing stopped. The answering machine turned on. Her sister's message ended, and the machine made its high-pitched beep.

And then there was heavy breathing.

"Tonight." The single word cleaved the silence, detonating her nerves. The machine clicked off. The tape whirred softly as it rewound.

Her adrenaline surged. Panic wiped out her thoughts. She had to run. Flee. Go somewhere, anywhere, and keep her daughter safe.

She looked at Claire, saw her daughter's lower lip quiver, the anxiety pinching her face. And she knew with dead certainty that she couldn't run. If this was Wayne, he'd only find them again. For Claire's sake, she had to end this terror now.

And if there was one thing she'd learned about her ex-husband, it was that he thrived on power and control. He wanted to see her run, plead, whimper with fear. And she'd be damned if she'd play his sick games.

She rose, her knees knocking so hard she could barely stand, and crossed the kitchen to the answering machine. She ejected the tape, slipped it into her pocket and disconnected the phone.

Then she grabbed her purse from the counter and

fumbled through her wallet for Detective Martinez's card. She found Luke Montgomery's number instead.

She hesitated. Should she call him? If the letter and phone calls were related to the casino attack, he would want to know.

But her priority was Claire, keeping her safe. Which meant reporting this to the police—no matter what Luke Montgomery might want.

Still, the memory of the skepticism in his eyes made her pause. He hadn't trusted her; that had been clear. He thought she'd sell her story to the highest bidder, even though she'd given him her word.

And maybe she was a fool to care, but there was something sad about a man that cynical, who thought that money always talked. And if she didn't call him now, she'd only confirm his jaded beliefs.

So maybe she should warn him. Maybe she should update him on this latest threat first and then inform the police.

And pray that whoever was watching them didn't see them go.

She met her daughter's frightened eyes, and a frigid pit formed in her gut. Claire was right to be afraid. Because if their watcher learned what she was up to, her daughter would pay the price.

The Las Vegas police were certainly thorough. Three hours later, Amanda still hunched on a folding metal chair in the Las Vegas Metropolitan Police station while Claire dozed on her lap. She'd turned over the evidence, given multiple statements, submitted fingerprints so they could exclude her prints from the note. Now several people crowded around her in the air-conditioned room—the detective she'd met in the casino, a petite police officer named Natalie Rothchild, several others whose names she couldn't recall.

And Luke Montgomery. He'd arrived shortly after she had, to her surprise. Now he sat in the chair beside her, the sleeves of his crisp white shirt rolled up, his dark forearms braced on his knees, listening intently while Natalie Rothchild summed up the case.

The police officer tucked her short brown hair behind her ears, then cleared her throat. "All right, then. In light of these developments, I think we have to consider the possibility that the ring isn't lost after all."

"Damn," Luke muttered.

Amanda glanced around at the circle of grim faces, confused. "What ring?"

Detective Martinez shifted his bulky frame in his seat. "We had a murder case recently—a woman named Candace Rothchild. You might have read about it in the news."

"Yes." She'd read up on the sensational case after she'd met Luke.

"She was Natalie's sister," he added.

"Oh." Amanda shifted her gaze to the other woman. "I'm sorry."

Natalie nodded. A pained look shadowed her eyes. "The night she was killed, Candace was wearing a diamond ring, a family heirloom we called the Tears of the Quetzal. We never found it, so we assumed it was lost. But we'll have to rethink that now."

Amanda frowned. "You think my note is related to that ring?"

"I think we have to consider that possibility, yes."

"But I just moved here. How could I possibly be involved?"

"That's what we need to find out. And it might not be related. But we can't rule it out, especially since the man who held you up demanded a ring. And that note is similar to the one my father received." She turned her head, spoke to one of the men. "Get that note to Lex Duncan at the FBI, will you?"

Amanda's head whirled. She gaped at the nodding men. Surely they were joking. She was tangled up in a diamond theft? It didn't make any sense.

She gave her head a sharp shake, tried to recall the facts of the case. From what she'd read, Luke had hosted a jewelry convention in his casino a few weeks back. Celebrities from around the globe had attended the glitzy event—including the casino heiress Candace Rothchild. Later that night she'd been murdered, her ring stolen. The priceless diamond ring—rumored to be under a bizarre curse promising the wearer love at first sight—had never been found.

Luke had originally been a suspect, although he'd later been cleared of the crime. She cut her gaze to his harsh profile, noted the rigid line of his jaw. No wonder he'd come here. He was as involved in this case as she was.

She pressed her hand to her throat, still unable to process it all. It was bad enough to think Wayne could be watching her. But a vicious murderer...

"There's something else I need to tell you," Natalie said gently.

Dazed, Amanda jerked her attention from Luke. The other police officers rose and began filing out. "I'm sorry. What?"

"Your ex-husband was released from jail last week."

Shock rippled through her. She tightened her hold on Claire. "But…Detective Martinez said he was in jail."

Natalie made a face. "I'm sorry. There was a computer glitch, and some of the data didn't get entered on time. Wheeler reported to his parole officer in Maryland yesterday, though, so you shouldn't have to worry about him."

"You don't know Wayne." He was clever. Cunning. And he knew her habits, her fears. She closed her eyes, felt her skin go cold. Her worst nightmare had just returned.

Natalie stood. "We've increased our patrols in your neighborhood, and we'll have someone monitor the house tonight in case anyone goes near that mailbox. We've also told Maryland to alert us if Wheeler breaks his parole."

It wouldn't do any good. Wayne had gotten around those measures before. A tight ball of terror knotted her gut.

Natalie shook her hand. "We'll be in touch."

"Thank you," she whispered, knowing there wasn't much else the police could do. She'd learned that fact back East.

"Claire, honey." She nudged her daughter gently to wake her. "It's time to go."

She roused her daughter, helped her to her feet, then left the room on quivering legs. Behind her, Luke and Natalie began to talk.

So Wayne was out of jail. He would come after her, if he hadn't already. He'd promised her he would. And if that weren't enough, she had a killer on her heels, demanding a ring she didn't have. Hysteria gurgled inside her. Could her life get any worse?

And what on earth should she do? Clutching Claire's small hand, she exited the building, then squinted in the blinding sun. She had to go home, warn Kendall. But then what? Should she leave town?

Would it do any good? Running from Wayne was hard enough. How could she flee an enemy she didn't know?

"Mommy," Claire said, her voice anxious.

Realizing she'd been squeezing Claire's hand, she relaxed her grip. "Don't worry. Everything's okay," she lied. She knelt, ignored the pavement sizzling her bare knees, and gave her daughter a hug. She buried her face in her hair, inhaled her little-girl scent, held her small, warm body tight against hers.

But a terrible dread lodged inside her, a wild, desperate fear that seeped like ice through her bones. How could she protect her daughter from a killer? She'd never felt more terrified in her life.

But she had to succeed. Claire's life was in her hands. She opened her eyes, smoothed the silky strands of hair from her daughter's cheeks, then eased her grip and rose.

"How about macaroni and cheese for dinner?" she suggested. This was definitely a comfort food night. "And then we'll watch a movie, maybe *Mary Poppins*. Would Brownie like that?"

Claire whispered to her bear, then held it up to her ear. Her big blue eyes met hers. "*The Little Mermaid,* too."

"Sure, we can do that." They might as well watch movies all night. No way would she fall asleep knowing a killer was lurking outside. She grabbed Claire's hand and stepped off the curb.

"Amanda, wait." She glanced back, surprised to see Luke Montgomery hurrying toward her, his black hair glinting in the sun.

He caught up to her and stopped. He glanced at Claire, then leveled his whiskey-brown eyes at hers. "We need to talk."

"Sure." Although she couldn't imagine what he'd have to say. She motioned to her green Honda Accord across the lot. "I parked in the shade. Why don't we talk over there?"

"All right." She started across the lot with Claire, and he slowed his pace to theirs. Without her high heels on, she was more aware of his height, the power in his fluid stride.

She slid a glance at the hard male planes of his face, that sexy, carnal mouth. His eyes captured hers, and a sudden tension sparked between them, igniting a flurry of nerves. She quickly turned away.

They stopped in the patch of shade beside her car. He leaned back against it, folded his muscled arms across his chest. His gaze caught hers again, touching off another rush of adrenaline, and she forced herself to breathe.

"What kind of security system do you have?" he asked.

"On the house?" She frowned, led Claire around the car to the rear passenger door, hoping the distance would quiet her nerves. "We don't have one, just locks on the windows and doors."

"That's what I figured." He turned to face her, propped his forearm on the roof, drawing her gaze to the black hair marching across his tanned arm. "If that killer's out there, you need better protection than that."

Her stomach clenched. "I know." But it would take time to get a security system installed—time she didn't have.

"I have a place you can stay," he said, and she raised

her brows. "A house. It's in a gated community on the north side of town. It has an alarm system, round-the-clock security guards. You'll be safe there."

She stared at him over the roof. He was offering her the use of his house? "That's nice of you, but—"

"I'm not doing it to be nice. Not entirely." The edge of his mouth quirked up. "You and your daughter need protection. I don't want any bad publicity right now. If you're in a safe place, the attacks will stop. It solves both our problems.

"The house is comfortable enough," he continued. "It has a pool, tennis courts, a home theater. If there's anything else you need, you can let me know."

Comfortable enough? He had to be joking. She'd seen pictures of the mansion in the tabloids. It put a sheikh's desert palace to shame. "Comfort isn't the issue."

"Then what is?"

She made an exasperated sound. "Well, for starters, I don't even know you."

He lifted one broad shoulder in a shrug. "You'd hardly see me. I spend most of my time in my penthouse. And it's only until they find this guy."

"Even so…" She shook her head, opened the car door for Claire. It was impossible, crazy. "What if the tabloids find out? Won't that make things worse?"

"I doubt they'll find out. They won't expect it, and I pay my staff not to talk. Although…" He drummed his fingers on the car roof, and a calculating look entered his eyes. "That's not a bad idea. We could spin it, play that angle up. Hell, the consortium might even approve."

"I'm afraid you've lost me."

"If the media thinks we're engaged, it would give

them something to speculate about besides the murder. I'd need you to attend a few events with me, though."

"Engaged?" Her jaw dropped. He wanted her to pose as his fiancée? "But…that's ridiculous. No one would believe it. I'm not even your type."

Amusement crinkled his eyes. "They'll believe whatever story we feed them. Besides…" His gaze dipped, making a long, heated slide over her breasts, and her heart fluttered hard. "I think I know my own type."

"Right." Her voice came out breathless, and her face turned warm. This was nuts. She had to get a grip and control herself before she totally embarrassed herself. "Except that if I'm in the news, Wayne and that murderer will know where I am for sure."

"But at least you'll have better security."

She couldn't argue that. She and Claire were vulnerable right now. She'd even dragged her sister into this mess. But moving into Luke's mansion…

"I appreciate the offer," she said carefully. "I really do. But I'll have to think about it."

His expression turned sharp. "You think I murdered Candace Rothchild? Is that the problem?"

"What? No, of course not." She ducked, helped Claire into her car seat to avoid his scrutiny. Truthfully, she didn't know what to think. According to the tabloids, Luke had argued with the murdered woman that night, and they'd had a tumultuous, romantic past. But the police had cleared him of the crime. And she couldn't imagine him killing anyone, considering how gentle he'd been with her.

But she was a lousy judge of men.

She straightened, flexed her wrist—a stark reminder of just how flawed her judgment was.

Luke's gaze stayed on hers. "I didn't do it. I despised the woman, but I didn't kill her. That's part of the problem, though. If they reopen the case, I'll be back in the news. The police might investigate me again."

"I'm sorry. It's just…this is pretty sudden. I need to think." She closed Claire's door, walked around the car to the driver's side. Luke straightened and stepped out of her way.

"You'd like the house. You both would," he said as she climbed inside. She nodded, closed the door, then rolled down the windows to let in air.

He bent down, putting his face just inches from hers. She tried to ignore the virile beard stubble coating his jaw, the disturbing effect of his riveting gaze. "It's a safe place, Amanda." His deep voice caressed her nerves. "No one will bother you there."

Except him. "Thank you. I really will think about it."

Of course she couldn't accept the offer. It was beyond ludicrous. She'd already moved in once with a man she'd barely known, and that had been a disaster. She couldn't compound her mistakes.

She backed out of her parking space and drove to the nearest exit. While she waited for a break in traffic, she glanced in the rearview mirror. Luke stood by a gleaming black Jaguar convertible, watching her with those arresting eyes.

She shivered. No wonder the women flocked to him. Just being near him had a devastating effect on her nerves.

And he was wrong about the media. Even if she agreed to the fake engagement, they would never buy it. She spotted a break in the traffic and gunned the car, anxious to leave Luke behind. She'd seen photos of his dates in the tabloids—gorgeous, voluptuous women, the kind who wore designer clothes, shoes that cost more than most people's mortgage payment. A-list women who vacationed on exotic beaches and sunbathed on yachts.

Whereas she was a high school history teacher. A single mother with a three-year-old child. And she couldn't forget that fact.

She sighed, changed lanes, then worked her way through the city streets toward home. That was the mistake she'd made with Wayne. She'd been flattered when he'd asked her out, impressed that a rich, charming man had showered attention on her. She hadn't cared about his money, but it had been so darned nice to have someone pamper her for once. All her life she'd worked to put food on the table, to keep sanity in their unstable lives. Wayne had made her feel sheltered, cared for. She'd even admired his self-control.

Big mistake. One she couldn't afford to repeat.

She turned into her sister's street, pushed thoughts of the past from her mind. She neared the house and slowed the car, and every cell in her body tensed. She inhaled, blew out a long, slow breath, trying to stay calm. But what if Wayne was nearby? What if the killer was here? Her knuckles turned white on the wheel.

She pulled into her driveway and idled the car, hardly able to breathe. She scanned the neighbors' bushes and yards, watched for movement around her house. Nothing. She pried her hand from the wheel, hit the button on the remote to open the garage door, checked the street in the rearview mirror.

Everything was fine. No one was there.

The garage door swung open, and she drove inside,

her pulse flaying her skull. God, she hated this fear, this constant anxiety, the need to listen, watch, run. She cut the engine and set the brake. Still scanning the garage, she unlatched her seat belt and opened her door.

The side door burst open. A masked man lunged toward her, a crowbar in hand.

She shrieked, slammed her door shut and hit the locks. Her heart rioting, her hands fumbling, she jammed the key back into the ignition. But the man leaped around the car and smashed Claire's window.

Claire wailed. Amanda's heart went berserk.

She cranked the engine, rammed the gearshift into Reverse, shaking so hard she couldn't think. She yanked off the brake, slammed the accelerator to the floor. The car rocketed out of the garage backward, shot down the driveway into the street—and crashed.

Amanda screamed, her voice merging with the din of twisting metal and shattering glass. The car jumped forward from the impact, hurling her against the steering wheel, and she gasped at the sharp jab of pain.

The car rocked backward again, then stopped. The sudden silence rang in her ears. Stunned, she looked up. The man in the garage ran off.

She swiveled around in panic. Claire still sat in her car seat, sobbing, clutching her bear, her face streaked with tears. But she was all right. She was all right. They'd both survived.

But who had she hit? She looked out the rear window. A cop emerged from his crumpled car.

She closed her eyes, rested her throbbing forehead against the steering wheel, ignored the blood trickling down her cheek. The cop banged on her door. She gestured for him to wait.

And the horror of it all washed through her. She'd nearly lost Claire. That man had tried to abduct her. She'd nearly failed to protect her child.

She sucked in her breath and knew she no longer had a choice. Whether she knew Luke or not didn't matter. They were moving into his mansion tonight.

Chapter 4

Luke had a reputation for being ruthless in business—a reputation he deserved. He crushed all opposition, never let emotions interfere with a decision and never lost sight of his goals.

Which didn't at all explain the turmoil now roiling through him, this odd hesitation to involve Amanda in his plans.

He prowled across his sunny patio toward the pool, the Italian tiles warming his bare feet. He watched Amanda steer her daughter through the sparkling blue water, the kid's arms buoyed by inflatable wings.

Bringing Amanda here made sense. She needed security, which he could provide. In exchange, she would lend him an air of stability, help pacify the consortium until they voted on the project next week. It was a logical arrangement, mutually beneficial—vital now that he'd read the morning news.

He scowled, skirted one of the twenty-foot Canary Island palm trees ringing the pool, tossed the offending newspaper onto a chair. He needed her help, all right. His project's success hinged on this plan.

Hell of a time for a crisis of conscience.

She glanced up from the pool just then and shielded her eyes from the sun. "Luke."

"Mind if I join you?"

"Of course not. Come on in." She steered her daughter to the side of the pool.

He dropped his towel on the chair and dove in, then swam underwater to where she stood in the shallow end. He surfaced near the others, shook the water from his eyes. The kid giggled and ducked behind her mother's back.

"Say hello to Mr. Montgomery," Amanda told her.

"Luke," he corrected.

Amanda smiled, her blue eyes warming, and his heart made a sudden lurch. "Say hello to Luke then."

The kid peeked out. "Luke then," she whispered and giggled again.

Luke grinned back and gently splashed her, and she squealed with delight. Claire was a miniature version of her mother with that angel-white hair and big blue eyes. A little shy, cute as hell.

Her mother wasn't cute. She was a knockout. Thick, dark lashes framed her dazzling eyes. Her hair was wet from the swim, slicked back, emphasizing the feminine lines of her face. Water glistened on her lips and shimmered in the hollow of her throat.

He looked at her shoulders, over the tantalizing cleavage bared by the scoop-necked suit. Water lapped over her breasts, bringing them in and out of focus like a desert mirage, tempting him to peel down that conservative suit, lick the sparkling drops from her skin.

Aware that he was staring, he jerked his mind to why he was here. "I've got news."

Her full lips pursed, and she glanced at Claire. "Let me get Claire settled down for a nap. It won't take long."

"Take your time. I'll swim some laps." He watched her maneuver her daughter to the steps. Water streamed from her shoulders and back as she climbed from the pool. His eyes followed in the water's wake, skimming her naked back, her perfect butt, the taut, creamy skin of her thighs.

She picked up a towel and quickly wrapped it around her waist. The modest gesture amused him, piquing his interest even more.

But it was an interest he couldn't indulge in right now. He plunged back into the water and began counting laps, relying on the exertion to settle his mind. A mile and a half later, his arms and shoulders tired, and the tension pounding in his temples eased. Feeling more controlled now, he touched bottom and waded to the side of the pool.

Amanda waited in a nearby lounge chair. She'd changed, and her snug, sleeveless T-shirt hugged her round breasts. Her hair had dried, and wispy blond tendrils fluttered around her face. Her shorts bared her elegant legs.

So much for regaining his focus.

He sighed, braced his hands on the edge of the pool and heaved himself out. He caught her eyes wandering over his shoulders and arms, down to his abdomen, and below. She bit her lip, looked away.

So she felt the attraction, too. Good to know, even if the timing sucked. He grabbed his towel, shook the water from his hair, then pulled up the chair next to hers.

Her blue eyes met his, and that unnerving sizzle jolted through him again. "I want to thank you again for letting us stay here," she said. "The house is beautiful. And this view…" She waved at the mountains beyond the golf course. "It's fabulous."

"You're comfortable then?"

She shot him a look of disbelief. "This place is amazing. It's like a palace. I've never stayed anywhere so nice."

He nodded absently, blotted the water still trickling down his jaw. "I talked to my security chief this morning, Matt Schaffer. He's engaged to Natalie Rothchild, the police officer you met yesterday."

"What did he say?"

"No one showed up at the mailbox last night."

Her forehead creased. "So they didn't catch the guy who attacked us."

"No, but the FBI thinks the note matches the one Natalie's father got. They won't know for sure until they run tests, but on the surface it looks the same."

Her face paled, making the freckles stand out on her nose. "So the man who tried to kidnap Claire… You're saying he might have been the killer?"

"Maybe."

Her eyes searched his. "You think he'll figure out where we are?"

He handed her the morning newspaper. She unfolded it, glanced at the headlines, and blanched even more. "Oh, God."

"Yeah." The lead story rehashed the missing ring

and murder, his possible role in the crime. Beneath that was a photo of Amanda with Claire.

"But how did they get this photo?" She sounded bewildered.

"Hell if I know."

She gnawed her lip. Stark fear shone in her eyes. "So he knows where we are now. He'll come after us for sure."

"He can't get in. Even a pro would have a hard time cracking this system. And I'm hiring extra guards, just to be safe.

"This was always a risk," he continued, wanting to reassure her. "I thought we'd have more time before the news broke, but it shouldn't affect our plan."

"Our plan?" She sounded numb.

"To pass you off as my fiancée. There's a charity event at the Rothchilds' tomorrow night. My investors will be there. If you're up to it, it's a good place to make your debut."

She passed her hand over her face, turned her gaze to his. "I'm sorry. I'm a little lost here. Investors in what?"

"A project I'm building—a casino and high-rise complex called the Phoenix. It was all set until the real estate market flatlined. Then Candace got murdered, and all hell broke loose." Every damned investor had threatened to bolt. "I've been making progress, getting the investors back on board, but they're still nervous. They're not going to sink money into this project if they think I'm going to jail."

She frowned. "What exactly do you want me to do?"

"Nothing hard. Just hang on my arm and smile, act unconcerned. If you're not worried about the rumors, it will calm them down. They vote on the project next week."

Her forehead furrowed, and for a moment she didn't speak. The warm breeze rustled the palm fronds overhead, dappling shadows over her face.

"Security's tight at these events," he added. "You'll be safe enough." But there was no guarantee. Unease wormed through his gut again, setting off that inconvenient feeling of guilt.

And he knew he had to be honest. No matter how important this project was, no matter how much he needed her help, he couldn't force her to risk her life.

"Look," he said. "You don't have to do this. I can send you somewhere else until this thing blows over—on an extended cruise or to some resort. You might feel safer that way."

Her troubled gaze met his. And then she rose, walked to the hedge along the patio wall. She stopped with her back to the pool and hugged her arms. She looked so lonely, so in need of protection that he had that damned urge to comfort her again.

He picked up his towel and joined her at the wall. For a long moment he just looked at the mountains beyond the golf course, their brown peaks shimmering in the rising heat. And the irony of his predicament made his lips curl. All his life, he'd stared at those mountains. When he was a kid in the slums, they'd seemed huge to him, formidable, like everything he wanted to become—powerful, bigger than the rest. And he'd vowed that someday he *would* be someone, that he'd have money, respect…revenge.

Now it was finally within his grasp. His plans would come to a head next week. But he couldn't put this woman's life at risk, no matter how important the goal.

Amanda turned to him then, and this close he could

see the fatigue tightening her eyes, the dark circles bruising her skin. She looked delicate, wounded, as if she hadn't slept in days.

"I'm serious," he told her. "I can have you and Claire out of here and halfway around the world by tonight."

She sighed. "Thanks, but it won't do any good."

"Sure it will."

"You don't understand." She looked toward the mountains again and flexed her wrist. "My ex-husband, Wayne… He was violent, volatile. I lived in fear of him for years. It was like living in a war zone. I was always on edge, afraid that something would set him off and make him explode. And I…I can't live like that anymore."

"But this isn't about your ex."

"Maybe not, but it doesn't matter. It's exactly the same thing. If this guy thinks I have the ring, he's not going to give up. No matter where I go, he'll follow me. I'll always be looking over my shoulder, wondering if this is the day he finds me, if this is the day he attacks. Wondering if he's watching, waiting."

She rubbed her arms, her eyes frightened, trying to be so brave it made Luke's chest hurt. And he couldn't resist the need building inside him, the need to defend her, protect her. Touch her.

He stepped close. He reached out slowly, giving her time to react, but she didn't flinch, didn't move away. He stroked the velvet skin of her jaw with his thumb, brushed the feminine line of her throat. She was so soft, so gentle. And yet, she was determined to stand her ground.

And something stirred inside him. Something beyond sympathy. Beyond the instinctive need to protect. The realization that this woman was different, special.

Her eyes turned dark. Her pulse raced against his thumb. He leaned closer, so close that his thighs brushed hers. Her warm breath feathered his face.

He knew he should let go, back away, put some space between them. He couldn't move.

His gaze dropped, traced the lush, sultry swell of her lips, then flicked back to her mesmerizing eyes. And a deep ache surged inside him, the need to pull her into his arms, fit that sweet, curving body to his, taste the provocative heat of her lips.

But this woman needed comfort, protection—not sex. He fisted his hand and stepped back.

"You're sure about this?" His voice rasped in the quiet air. "It's not too late to change your mind."

"I'm sure. I'll stay." Her voice was as throaty as his.

"Good." They were committed now, their bargain struck—until his deal went through and the killer was found. "Then I'll pick you up tomorrow at nine."

She hesitated. "I need to check with Kendall first and see if she can get the night off. Claire might not stay with anyone else, especially in a strange house."

"I'll clear it with her boss. She can go on paid vacation for the next few weeks."

"All right then."

He frowned, wishing he could reassure her, wanting to erase the concern from her face. But there were no guarantees. And he didn't trust himself to stay.

Before he could reconsider, he strode across the patio to the house, then paused at the door and looked back. She still stood by the hedge watching him, her eyes worried.

And he knew he had to be careful. There was something different about this woman. Something too compelling. If he didn't watch out, she'd slip under his guard, become far more than a means to clinch the Phoenix deal.

And that was a risk he couldn't afford.

Amanda stood beneath the chandelier in the private ballroom of the Rothchild Grand Casino, her sister's dire warnings about Luke still ringing in her ears. He was an incorrigible playboy, cutthroat in business, possibly even a murderer—a dangerous, worldly wolf to her naive and innocent lamb.

But dangerous or not, he'd been the epitome of charm tonight. He'd introduced her to his investors, hovered attentively at her side, acting the enamored fiancé to the hilt.

He leaned close, and the scent of his warm male skin, the sight of his white teeth flashing in his handsome face made her heart rate climb. "Champagne?" he asked, and his deep voice rumbled through her nerves.

"Sure." Now that she'd survived the first round of introductions without a major faux pas, she could relax.

Luke motioned to a passing waiter and scooped a drink from his tray. The motion tightened his black tuxedo jacket across his broad back. She admired his freshly shaven jaw, the strong lines of his corded neck. And images paraded through her mind like an erotic slideshow—his biceps flexing as he surged from the pool, the dark hair arrowing down his muscled chest. And that delirious moment when his eyes turned to molten gold and she thought that he might kiss her... She inhaled, pressed her hand to her belly to subdue the jitters rising inside.

He turned to her, held out the drink and their eyes locked. And tension ignited between them again, that electric spark of desire. She took the drink with trembling hands, struggled to act composed. They were only pretending, for goodness' sake. The worst thing she could do was start spinning fantasies about Luke. She'd end up mortifying them both.

But just one glance from those carnal eyes and everything inside her went wild.

"I see someone I need to talk to by the bar," he told her.

She cleared the thickness from her throat. "I'll wait here." She could use a moment to compose herself.

He nodded. "I'll only be a minute."

She sipped her drink, watched him work his way across the room. Women latched onto his arm like long-lost friends. Men greeted him with deference and shook his hand. These were the high rollers of Las Vegas, the elite. And they all kept their eyes on Luke.

She drained her glass, hummed to the piano music lilting in the background. A burst of laughter broke out nearby. Waiters in crisp white jackets wove past, scooping up discarded glasses and refreshing drinks.

How many events like this had she attended with Wayne? Not that he'd moved in quite these circles, but they'd been lofty enough. And at every party, he'd worked the crowd, charming clients with that smarmy smile, arranging illicit affairs with the wives. And she'd had to smile through her teeth, play the role of the devoted wife—until she'd finally squirreled away enough money to escape.

A waiter materialized at her elbow. "Another drink, ma'am?"

Goosebumps rose on her arms at the sound of his voice. She cut her gaze to his face, but he just stood there, his expression polite.

She pulled in a breath, forced herself to relax. She didn't know him. He was just a waiter doing his job, wanting to swap out her empty glass. Feeling foolish, she thanked him, exchanged her flute for the full one left on his tray. He bent, picked up a stray glass from a table and strolled away.

She sipped her champagne, determined not to revert to survival mode and start scanning the crowd. She had to stop jumping at shadows. Luke had promised she'd be safe here. She had to forget her fears and calm down.

She looked for Luke, spotted him talking to a gorgeous brunette. Jenna Rothchild. Amanda had met her earlier. The woman clung to his arm, her pose intimate, suggestive, and whispered into his ear. Luke flashed her a wicked smile, then turned to watch her walk away.

Amanda's head throbbed. So much for the enamored fiancé.

But she didn't care. She didn't. Her relationship with Luke was an act, a ploy. He could flirt as much as he liked.

She didn't plan to stand here and watch, though. She drank more champagne, lifted her wrist to check the time, but she'd left her watch at the house. No sporty watch, no bulky purse allowed tonight, her sister had decreed, only the small, sequined clutch that matched her borrowed dress.

Suddenly weary, she pasted a smile on her face, nodded to one of the investors—a balding man she'd met earlier—and wandered toward the corner where the pianist played. She glanced around for a chair, did a double take when she spotted the pianist's face. Silver Rothchild, the former teen pop star. Her career had fizzled as she'd aged, but Amanda had always loved her songs. And goodness, that music she was playing took her back—back to a time when she'd had dreams, her whole life still ahead.

Before she'd met Wayne.

She grimaced and pushed away that depressing thought. She hummed a few bars of the song, glanced at Silver again and noticed how exhausted she looked. Her face was pale. Dark smudges shadowed her eyes. Amanda could relate. She hadn't slept well in days.

A wave of dizziness hit her, and she pressed her hand to her pounding head. Talk about tired. And this headache was getting worse. She pushed back the fatigue, drank the last of her champagne, then glanced around for Luke, but he still chatted across the room.

A man stepped into her path, his dark eyes hard on hers, and her heart made a sudden swerve. But it was just the waiter, the same one she'd seen earlier. She was getting paranoid now.

And Lord, she was tired. Her head whirled. The entire room seemed to tilt. She set the empty glass on his tray, but it fell off and bounced on the rug.

"I've got it," he murmured.

"Thanks," she said, her voice slurred. Oh, God. Was she drunk? That was all Luke needed, for his fiancée to act like a fool. But how could she be drunk? She'd only had two tiny flutes of champagne.

Her face grew hot. Sweat trickled down her scalp and beaded her upper lip. The waiter still stood there, looking expectantly at her, and she used her purse to fan her face.

What did he want? Why was he staring at her like that? She lurched past him, searching for the ladies' room, desperate to find a place to sit down.

But her heart started to race. Her skin felt clammy,

then chilled. She staggered, bumped into the wall, narrowly missing a huge gilded frame. She paused, her face burning now. How could she be sweating when she felt so cold?

She fumbled with the clasp on her clutch purse, searched for one of the tissues she'd stuck inside. The purse was empty.

She frowned. She'd folded up three blue tissues and tucked them inside, next to her lipstick and blush. And she hadn't opened her purse since she'd left the house.

Confused, she veered to a nearby table, grabbed a cocktail napkin from the stack, knocking the rest to the floor. Too dizzy to pick them up, she dabbed her streaming face.

"Ma'am?" someone asked. She turned her head, and the waiter's face wove into view. "Do you need help?"

"Help?" Was that her voice coming from so far away? She stared at him, shocked when his face morphed into Luke's. She blinked, and the waiter's vaguely Hispanic face reappeared.

Someone grabbed her arm. "No," she whispered, and the waiter laughed. Luke's golden eyes seared into hers. The room faded, began to twirl.

And then everything went black.

Chapter 5

Her eyelids refused to open. A dull pounding buffeted her head. *Claire. Where was Claire?* She had to make sure she was safe.

Amanda wrenched open her eyelids, then squinted at the blast of bright sun. Her gaze landed on the copper-colored bedspread, the Navajo rug on the wall. Luke's mansion. She'd made it home. She slumped against the pillows in relief.

"You're awake." Luke's deep voice rumbled from the corner of the room.

She turned her head as he heaved himself from an armchair, then prowled across the room to her side. His thick hair was tousled, his eyes somber. He had on loose, faded jeans, a wrinkled shirt that he'd left undone, inviting glimpses of his muscled abs. Morning whiskers darkened his jaw, giving him a virile, gunslinger look.

She sank deeper into the pillows and closed her eyes. He looked sexy as sin, conjuring thoughts of torrid nights and sweaty sheets. Whereas she probably had raccoon eyes from her makeup and rat's nest hair.

"How do you feel?" he asked.

As if she'd been dragged through a garbage chute. "Not great." She turned her head to the side, winced at the pulsing pain. "What time is it?"

He perched on the edge of her bed near her hip, and she scooted over to give him more room. "Noon. You've been out since I brought you back last night."

She shut her eyes, massaged the ache between her brows. Her eyes felt gritty, and she desperately needed to bathe. "Where's Claire?"

"In the kitchen with your sister. We told her you were tired and needed to sleep. She left you something, though."

Amanda opened her eyes, saw Brownie propped on the pillow beside her head and a huge rush of love warmed her heart. She picked up the bear, pressed the threadbare fur to her cheek. "I hope she didn't see me come in."

"She was asleep."

"Thank goodness." The last thing she wanted to do was frighten Claire. But what must Luke think of her? She'd passed out at the reception, created a scene. "I'm so sorry," she said. "I didn't mean to embarrass you last night."

He lifted one massive shoulder, his expression inscrutable. "Don't worry about it."

"But people must be talking."

"It doesn't matter."

"Of course it does." He'd wanted to avoid bad publicity and give the impression of settling down. Instead, she'd made things worse. "The investors... They must have seen me." And who knew what they'd think?

"We'll adjust." His eyes wandered over her face, her lips. She felt the heat rising from his body, the tantalizing scent of his hair. She fiddled with the bear, her breathing suddenly labored, her heart fluttering in her chest. Lord, he was sexy. The sheer maleness of him made her body hum.

She peeked under the covers, relieved to see she had on her knee-length T-shirt. Kendall must have undressed her. At least she hoped it was Kendall and not Luke. Her face turned hot at the thought.

"So what happened?" he asked.

Good question. She set down the bear and frowned, trying hard to think back. "I'm not sure. I felt fine, a little tired. I saw you talking to Jenna Rothchild."

She eyed his chiseled mouth, the lean, masculine planes of his face. She couldn't blame Jenna for flirting. If he weren't so far out of her league she'd be tempted herself. "I had some champagne, and then I felt dizzy."

"How much did you drink?"

"Two glasses, hardly enough to make me drunk. Plus, I'd eaten a lot of hors d'oeuvres."

Brackets deepened around his mouth. "You think it was food poisoning?"

"I doubt it. That wouldn't make me black out. And I didn't feel sick, just dizzy and tired."

His eyes narrowed, and she could tell he was flipping through possibilities, calculating the odds. "Had you taken any pills? Anything that could have reacted with the alcohol?"

"Nothing. Not even an aspirin." He slanted his head, his eyes turning grimmer yet, and the sudden realization of what he was thinking took her aback. "You think it was drugs."

"They can knock you out fast."

"But that's ridiculous. Who would want to drug me at the gala? The gunman wasn't there."

He rose, paced to the window, then stood facing out, his hands braced low on his hips.

"Luke?" He didn't answer, and her voice rose. "Why would anyone there want to hurt me?" What kind of mess was she in?

He turned and met her gaze. "To get you out of the picture, cause the investors to balk. This project will hurt the Rothchilds' business. Harold's trying to stop it from going through."

"Even so… You really think he'd drug me? Isn't that extreme?"

"He's done worse. In fact, I should have expected a move like this. There's a lot at stake here. He's probably getting desperate by now."

Her mind reeled. This was all she needed. She had a murderer on her heels, an abusive ex-husband who'd vowed to hunt her down—and now a deranged businessman might be drugging her drinks.

She had to admit that the drug explanation made sense, though. That dizziness had come over her fast. And there'd been something about that waiter's voice… But he couldn't be the same man who'd attacked her in the casino. Why would he be at the Rothchilds' event?

For that matter, Luke could have drugged her. She eyed the tight set of his jaw, the intelligence in his amber eyes. She really knew nothing about him, except the little she'd gleaned from the news.

And what if the rumors were true? What if he had

murdered Candace Rothchild and was now after the ring? Just before she'd blacked out, she had seen his face.

But that was absurd. If Luke had wanted to harm her, he'd have done it here, in his house, not in a public place. And certainly not in front of the investors he hoped to impress.

She rubbed the ache pulsing between her brows, struggling to sort through the confusion. Luke wouldn't hurt her. He wasn't a brute, not like Wayne. He was cynical and tough in business, but he'd been nothing but gentle with her.

So had Wayne at the start.

She flexed her wrist, trying not to go off the deep end and imagine the worst. Besides, there was another explanation for her blackout, one that had nothing to do with drugs.

One she dreaded even more.

She glanced around, spotted the sequined clutch on a chair, and her heart struck an uneven beat. She didn't want to look, but she had to find out the truth.

She tossed off the covers and rose, tugged her long T-shirt over her hips. Then she slowly advanced on the purse.

Her pulse pounded as she picked it up. She undid the clasp, hardly able to breathe. She jerked the sides apart. Her heart faltered. The tissues were there, tucked next to her lipstick, exactly how she'd placed them last night. Her hand rose to her throat.

"What's wrong?" Luke asked.

Her purse had been empty. Those tissues had been gone. But then how had they reappeared? "Nothing. I thought I lost my lipstick, that's all."

She set down the purse, her hands shaking. Had she imagined that they'd disappeared? Her mother had hallucinated, suffered from dizzy spells and blackouts...

She thought of the waiter morphing into Luke and back and quickly blocked off the thought. No. This couldn't be happening. She wouldn't let it. If she had inherited her mother's mental illness, she might have to give up Claire.

But what else could have happened? Who had moved the tissues, and why? The only people who'd been near her purse were her sister, Claire and Luke.

She swallowed hard, battled the hysteria surging inside her. She didn't know which was worse—thinking someone had drugged her or losing her mind.

Luke stalked toward her from across the room. She looked up and met his eyes. "I think... I was just overly tired." She made her voice firm. "And then the champagne... I'm sure that's all it was."

He stopped. Deep lines wrinkled his brow. "Do you want me to call a doctor?"

"No." The last thing she wanted was a doctor documenting this.

"He could do a blood test, find out if you'd been drugged."

And what if the answer was no? "I just need to rest. Really. I'll be fine."

"You're sure?"

"Yes." He moved closer, tipped up her chin, and his rough fingers tingled her skin. He studied her with narrowed eyes, as if to discern the truth. She struggled to look convinced.

"You'd better be all right," he said. "You scared the hell out of me last night."

He'd worried about her? She blinked, touched. She couldn't remember the last time anyone had worried about her. She'd always been the responsible one, the dependable one, the one who'd had to take charge and cope.

"Thank you," she murmured. "For everything. For bringing me back here, for helping—"

"Shh. Forget it." He pressed his thumb to her lips. The slight touch set off a storm of sensations, turning her insides to liquid heat. His hand slid to her cheek, cradled her jaw. His eyes didn't move from hers.

The moment stretched. She couldn't think. She was lost in his hot, hot eyes. He slanted his head, tilted her jaw up and she dropped her gaze to his mouth.

Would he kiss her? Her pulse raced. Excitement hammered her nerves. She tried to swallow, but her throat refused to work.

And then his lips touched hers and her heart jackhammered to life.

His lips were warm, smooth. Pleasure sizzled and rushed through her veins. She gripped his steel-hard arms, slid her palms up his powerful neck, thrilled to the erotic rasp of his jaw.

He felt so strong, so rough, so male. She wanted him closer, wanted that tough, muscled body hard against hers.

As if reading her mind, he tugged her against him, then prodded her lips with his tongue. She shuddered at the sensual invasion, at the deep, pulsing hunger she could barely contain.

He tasted like sin, her darkest temptation, a lure to excitement that she'd never known. The warm, male scent of him ignited her senses. The taste of him shorted her brain. And a sudden urgency consumed her, a desperate need to pull him close. She wanted his hands on her breasts, her naked skin. She wanted to throw off caution and live.

He groaned, widened his stance. The thick, massive feel of him scorched through her blood. She tightened her grip on his neck, bringing her aching breasts tighter against his chest. And still it wasn't enough.

But he stopped, pushed himself away, and she swayed at the sudden loss. And for several long seconds he just stared at her, his eyes glittering with hunger, arousal. Regret?

She blinked, dazed, tried to think through the thick fog of lust. What had come over her? She never acted that impulsive. And the door was open. Claire could come in at any time. She glanced at the doorway, appalled.

"I, uh…" He grimaced, lifted his hands, as if to ward her off. "You'd better rest."

"Right." Her face flamed. Her behavior mortified her. What must he think of her now?

His frown deepened. He inched closer to the door. "About the investors. We'll figure something out." He strode to the door, glanced back. His hot eyes blazed into hers. "And Amanda… Don't worry. I'll keep you safe."

He fled the room, and she sank onto the bed, her whole world spinning apart. What had just happened? How could a kiss affect her like that? She'd never felt such brazen urgency, so frantically turned on in her life.

Sex with Wayne had been tepid at best, revolting later on. She'd assumed that the problem was her, that she wasn't the physical type. Wayne had told her as much.

But that kiss… Dear God. She closed her eyes, pressed her hand to her still-throbbing lips, unable to believe her response.

Luke said he'd keep her enemies at bay—but who would protect her from herself?

As mistakes went, that kiss ranked up with the big ones.

Luke paced across the kitchen two nights later, watching Amanda at the table with Claire. He'd had no business touching Amanda. He'd only intended to offer comfort and calm his raging fear. Because the thought that someone had drugged her… His blood still congealed at the thought.

But giving comfort was one thing. Surrendering to those soft, sweet lips had been totally out of line.

He pivoted at the sink, stalked back toward the table, listening to the lilt of her voice. Even worse, no matter how many numbers he'd crunched, no matter how hard he'd worked in the past two days, he couldn't get her out of his head. He kept veering back to those warm, moist lips, the erotic brush of her breasts. That kiss had left him so knotted up that he'd do anything to touch her again.

Which was crazy. She wasn't even his type. He dated fast, jaded women. Women out for a night of hot sex. Amanda was too innocent, too vulnerable. She even had a kid.

She glanced up as he passed her again and blushed. *Blushed.* He shoved his hand through his hair, appalled. He didn't get involved with women who blushed. He'd lost his friggin' mind.

"Time for bed," she told her daughter. She rose, bent to help Claire from her chair, and his gaze zeroed in on her hips. She wore those shorts again, the ones that hugged her lush behind, exposing the tempting skin of

her thighs. And images flashed through his mind—
Amanda naked, stretched seductively over his bed,
dressed in nothing but a pair of high heels.

"Say good-night to Luke," she said, and he jerked his
mind from that scene.

"'Night, Luke." Claire trotted over and lifted her
bear. "Give Brownie a kiss."

"A kiss?" Caught off guard, he frowned at the scruffy
bear. But the kid was watching him with those huge,
blue eyes, and he hated to let her down. Feeling awk-
ward, he took the bear, pressed it to his cheek, then
flipped it into the air. It spun, started down headfirst, and
Claire made a startled gasp. He caught it on his knee,
juggled it several times like a soccer ball and launched
it back in the air. He snagged it on the down curve and
handed it to Claire.

Her eyes were wide, her mouth open. But then she
giggled, clutched the bear and ran back to her mom.

Amanda's eyes crinkled. Her lips curved into a
smile—a warm, easy smile that softened his heart. Not
his type, he reminded himself firmly. He turned, tracked
those killer legs as she sauntered away, mesmerized by
the swing of her hips.

When she'd disappeared from view, he leaned
against the counter and crossed his arms. Okay, this was
getting out of hand. He prided himself on his self-
control. Hell, he was famous for it. So why was she getting to him?

He frowned out the window at the darkening sky. If
she were different, he'd indulge in a brief affair. That
always got a woman out of his system and took the edge
off his sexual needs.

But there was something special about Amanda,

something he'd felt from the start. She threatened his distance, kicked up feelings he'd long suppressed.

And that was dangerous.

He gave his head a hard shake. He only had one more week until the consortium voted. One more week to masquerade as her fiancé. He could control himself until then.

Determined to regain his focus, he crossed the room to his wine vault, selected a bottle of *Riserva* he'd picked up in Tuscany the previous spring. He popped the cork, set the bottle on the counter to breathe while he waited for her to come back.

She strolled into the kitchen a moment later, then started gathering her papers into a pile.

"What are you working on?" he asked to get his mind off the intriguing way her breasts swayed as she reached for a paper that fell.

"My teaching credential." She set the wayward paper on the stack. "I need to get it validated in Nevada. They have a reciprocal agreement with Maryland, so I don't need to retake the tests. I just have to file the forms."

He pulled two wine glasses from the cupboard and held them up. "Wine?"

"Thanks, that would be nice."

He set down the glasses, watched as she stuffed Claire's crayons into the box. The overhead lamp made her blond hair shine and highlighted the curve of her cheeks. "What do you teach?"

"High school history." Her gaze met his. "I love your casino, by the way. You did an amazing job on the lobby."

He shrugged. "I didn't do it. I told the interior designer to make it look like Rome, then left the rest to her."

"Well, it's wonderful…magical. Ancient Rome must have looked exactly like that."

A wistful smile softened her face, and another spurt of warmth curled through his chest. He realized that he liked pleasing her, liked basking in her approval.

He scowled, turned back to the wine. Since when did he care what anyone thought? He worked alone, rarely asked for opinions. The only approval that mattered was his.

"Speaking of casinos, we need to make another appearance together." He poured the wine, crossed to the table and handed her a glass. "I'd like to do it soon. The consortium meets again early next week to review the final plans."

"All right."

"We should probably include Claire this time. She'll help us look more settled." Especially with the rumors now swirling around. Half of Vegas thought Amanda had an addiction that made her black out at the gala. The rest believed he'd tried to do her in.

But there was no point worrying her with that.

"I'm not sure about Claire." She sat and sipped her wine, her expression doubtful. "She gets shy around strangers, especially if we go somewhere new. Could we invite them here instead?"

He lowered himself into the chair next to hers. "I don't see why not." In fact, it was a good idea. It would give them a more domestic look. He leaned back in the chair, sipped the rich, dark wine, tried to ignore the tempting scent of her skin. "There are six investors, their wives and us. Fifteen people. I'll contact the caterer first thing."

"I don't mind cooking. In fact, I'd like to." She glanced around, and her lips turned up. "You have a fabulous kitchen to work in. And I make pretty good Mexican food—unless you want something fancier."

"No, Mexican's great." And having her cook would add to the homey look. "You're sure you don't mind?"

"I need to do something. I can't just sit here and worry all day."

The anxiety in her voice caught his attention. "Has something else happened?"

"No." She shook her head, but her eyes didn't quite meet his. "It's just the stress, not knowing where the killer is. There hasn't been any word?"

"Last I heard they were still waiting for the lab report."

She nodded, looked away, but this close he could see the fatigue shadowing her eyes. He took a swallow of wine, still studying her face. She was worried, no doubt about it. "You're sure there's not a problem?"

"No, nothing. Everything's fine."

He didn't buy it. She looked as if she hadn't slept in days. But he'd couldn't force her to talk. He nodded toward the papers stacked near her glass, decided to lighten the mood. "So you've never been to Rome?"

"I've never been anywhere. I've never even left the country."

"Why not?"

She shrugged. "Money, life. When I was younger, my mother...wasn't well. She couldn't work, and the disability checks didn't go too far, so I worked to help pay the rent. Then Kendall left for Vegas, and I stayed to help my mom."

He raised a brow. "That doesn't seem fair."

"Kendall sent money, and she came home when she could. Later she offered to move back so I could leave. But it didn't seem right to make her give up her dream. I mean, you can only dance when you're young, right? And I could study any time."

He didn't agree, but nodded for her to go on.

"I didn't mind teaching," she added. "It wasn't as exciting as being an archaeologist, but I liked the kids, and I had enough time off to take care of my mom."

He frowned. Her childhood sounded a lot like his with a mother who couldn't work. And no matter what she said, he doubted her sister had helped much. Amanda had probably taken charge of her mother like she now did Claire.

Disturbed by that thought, he drained his wine, then rose and paced to the sink. It was better if he didn't get involved with her, didn't know her past. It made her too sympathetic, too real.

Too damn hard to resist.

But when she came up behind him, he had to ask. "So where did Wheeler come in?"

She didn't answer at first. She rinsed her glass, wiped her hands, then finally leaned against the counter and sighed. "I met him after my mother died. I was planning to go to graduate school so I could study archaeology and get a job in the field. But he kept pressuring me to move in with him.

"I didn't want to. I hardly knew him. But then…well, I got pregnant, and I didn't want Claire to grow up without a father like I did." She grimaced. "Obviously, he wasn't the man I thought."

"No." He knew Wheeler's type. He'd seen a few violent men when he was growing up—bullies who fed their egos by terrorizing the weak. They were all about power, control. In fact, Wheeler had probably knocked her up just to keep her in his control.

That thought needled him, and he clenched his jaw. He didn't like knowing she'd suffered abuse at the hands of a scumbag. He didn't like knowing she lived in fear of the man.

And he sure as hell didn't like how she stood watching him with those big blue eyes, looking too damn defenseless as she clutched her wrist. His hold on his temper slid. "What happened to your wrist?"

"Nothing."

Like hell it was. "And that's why you hold it all the time?"

She flattened her lips, as if reluctant to talk, but then she let out a heavy sigh. "It was Wayne. He flew into a rage and broke it." Her eyes filled with remembered fear. "I found drugs in the house and confronted him. It was dumb. I never should have challenged him like that."

His mouth thinned. He didn't want to picture it. He didn't want to think of her cowering before that thug. And if he ever got his hands on Wheeler... Anger blazed through his gut.

"That's when I knew I had to leave," she added. "I didn't want drugs or violence around Claire."

That fit. She'd cared for her mom, sacrificed for her sister. And now she protected her child. But who'd ever protected her?

He caught hold of her injured wrist. She tugged back, but he stroked the delicate skin of her wrist with his thumb, felt the frantic beat of her pulse. And emotions swirled inside him. Respect, admiration, desire.

He slowly lifted her wrist, pressed his mouth to the sensitive skin, heard the sudden catch in her breath. Her seductive scent wrapped through his mind.

"Luke..." she whispered.

"I know." His voice came out too deep. "It's a bad idea."

"Very bad." Her pulse sped under his thumb. Her gaze didn't budge from his.

Get out, he urged himself. *Don't let this happen.* He didn't want to get involved with her. He didn't want to know her worries, her pain.

And he sure as hell didn't want to hear her plead for his touch, watch her eyes turn blurry with need or sink into that warmth and make her his.

She tugged her arm. He let her go. "I can't," she said, sounding desperate. "It's too complicated. Claire... There's too much else going on."

"Right." *Distance.* That was what he'd wanted. That was what he'd come for—to forget this attraction, to regain control, to prove that he could resist.

To stay detached.

But as he stared into her eyes, his gut roiling with hunger, he had a feeling it was already too damned late.

Chapter 6

The cilantro had disappeared.

Amanda stared into the refrigerator, unwilling to believe her eyes. She'd put it on the top shelf, right next to the artichoke dip. So where on earth had it gone?

She pawed through the vegetable drawers, her anxiety rising, then checked behind the enchiladas and rice. But the cilantro was nowhere in sight.

She straightened, pushed the refrigerator door closed with her hip and tried to keep herself calm. Okay. She knew she'd bought it. She'd ticked it off her grocery list. She remembered putting it on that shelf. But then how had it disappeared?

A sliver of dread trickled through her, but she struggled not to overreact. So she was acting a little bizarre these days, getting absentminded. She'd left her wallet in the bathroom, her comb in the silverware drawer.

She'd turned off lights, only to later find them switched back on.

But that didn't mean she had a mental illness. Anyone would forget things under this kind of stress.

She barely ate. She hardly slept, thanks to that awful paranoia that nagged her again, the feeling that someone was watching...waiting. And when she did give into exhaustion and nod off, memories of Luke invaded her dreams, leaving her breathless and aching with need.

"Mom. Help me," Claire called from the table, where she was coloring clothes for her paper doll.

"Not right now. We need to run to the store. I forgot something, and the guests will be here soon." She glanced at her watch, then gasped. Yikes. It was later than she'd thought. She had to get that cilantro fast.

She grabbed her purse from the counter, hustled Claire from the table to the garage and set the alarm. Luke wouldn't approve of the errand. Neither would Kendall. They'd both urged her not to budge from the house. But there was a grocery store just outside the entrance to the gated community. She could get there and back in fifteen minutes tops.

She strapped Claire into her car seat, backed quickly out of the garage. It felt good to get out, she decided moments later as she followed a gardening truck down the street. Luke's house was gorgeous—like a luxury resort—but after nearly a week, the confinement was starting to chafe.

She kept the windows rolled down, and the warm desert breeze ruffled her hair. Despite her current danger, she had to admit that she liked Nevada. She liked the wide-open spaces, the mountains jutting against the brilliant blue sky. There was something adventurous about the west. Even the air seemed to pulse with excitement, as if anything were possible here. It was a great place to start a new life—or it would be, once she escaped her current mess.

The supermarket sat in a small, modern strip mall just outside the community's gates. She found a parking space close to the cart return and rushed Claire into the store. She just prayed that they had cilantro, or she'd have to drive across town.

"I'm cold," Claire said, shivering in the air-conditioned store.

"I know. So am I. We'll hurry." She hustled her through the produce section, giving wide berth to a bin of peanuts that would trigger an allergic reaction in Claire. To her relief, there was plenty of cilantro. She shoved a fresh bunch into a plastic bag, grabbed a *jicama* to slice up for the dip. Seconds later, she'd led Claire through the checkout line, then exited to a blast of dry heat.

She pulled out her keys and checked her watch. Oh, God. She had to rush. Taking a firm grip on Claire's hand, she hurried up the row toward her car.

It was gone.

She stopped, whirled around, glanced up and down the row. This had to be the right spot. She'd parked by the cart return, right where a blue Corvette now sat. Bewildered, she scanned the spaces again, then walked between the cars to the next row. But there was still no sign of the car.

Where could it have gone? Had someone stolen it? But who'd take her old Honda with all the BMWs around? The repair shop had done a great job fixing the damage from that accident, but it was still hardly a prize.

"Mom," Claire complained, and she realized she was squeezing her hand.

"I'm sorry, honey. I just can't find our car." She turned in another circle, frantically searching the lot. And then she spotted it two rows away—nowhere near the cart return.

Her heart fumbled a beat. Her breath grew shallow and fast. She didn't remember parking there, had no memory of it at all. But no one could have moved it. No one else had a key.

Still clutching Claire's hand, she warily walked toward the car, feeling as if she were approaching a bomb. Dread pounded her skull. Her palms moistened with sweat. The car had Maryland plates on the brand-new bumper, Claire's car seat in the back. It was hers, all right. And it was locked.

But how could she not remember parking it here?

Her head buzzing, she unlocked the doors, buckled Claire in her seat and started home. Sprinklers swished on the nearby golf course. Laughing children bicycled past. She drove down the road like a zombie, her eyes glued straight ahead, too numb to process it all.

Still dazed, she parked the car in the garage, carried the groceries into the house, trying to focus on the evening ahead. Luke was depending on her to make a good impression tonight, and she couldn't mess up again. She'd think about the lost car and missing cilantro later, after the guests had gone.

She rinsed the cilantro, put it in the colander to drain, went to get the jalapeños from the fridge. She swung the door open, then froze.

The cilantro was back. Right where she'd left it on the shelf.

Her head felt light. The air turned hot and thick. She whipped around, searched the kitchen for signs of intrusion. But the windows were closed. Claire's paper dolls and crayons sat undisturbed at her place. Everything was fine.

Except for her.

Dear God. She was losing her mind.

Something was bothering Amanda.

Luke studied her as she fidgeted with the napkins on the patio table and smiled at Fletcher Coddington, their last, lingering guest. He doubted anyone else had noticed how nervous she was. She'd been the perfect, gracious hostess all night—smiling, keeping the conversation going, making sure everyone stayed comfortable and involved.

And the investors had fallen for her hard. They'd devoured the food she'd made, listened avidly to her stories about local history. Even Claire had behaved like a model child, giving him a stable, domestic appearance.

A car door slammed in the distance, and Amanda's head jerked up. His eyes narrowed. That was it, right there—the way she jumped at routine noises, the way her eyes tightened with the same anxious look he'd seen on that surveillance tape. All evening long her voice had been a little too high, her smile too bright.

Something was wrong, all right, and he intended to find out what. But first he had to get Fletcher Coddington to leave.

He headed toward her, and she glanced up. She straightened, her eyes going wide.

"You must be tired," he said smoothly. He slid his

arm around her waist and pulled her soft, curving body against his.

She stiffened. "I...I'm fine."

"You're sure?" He leaned down and nuzzled her neck, and she didn't quite stifle her gasp.

The hug was for show, part of the charade they'd been playing all night. But the scent of her skin, the feel of her full, round breasts brushing his arm sent a jolt of heat through his blood.

"Luke," she whispered when he nibbled her jaw. "Fletcher will see."

"I hope so." He moved his mouth to her ear, inhaled the aroma of her perfume. "I'm trying to make him leave."

It worked. Coddington set down his whiskey tumbler and glanced at his watch. "Montgomery, it's been a pleasure."

Amanda extracted herself from his arms and rushed to their guest. "I'm so sorry your wife couldn't make it tonight."

Coddington offered her his arm, and Luke followed them through the house. Amanda kept up the chatter until they reached the door.

"You'll have to stop by and see my arrowhead collection," Coddington told her. "I used to dig around the *pishkuns* in Montana when I was young. They frown on that now—can't dig in historical places, you know. I'll probably donate them to a museum some day."

"I'd love to see them," she said, sounding sincere, and Luke frowned at a sudden thought. They'd never discussed their eventual breakup, or exactly how long they'd keep up this charade. But they'd have to continue at least until that killer was found, and Amanda was safe.

Coddington turned to him then. "I take it you heard about the protests?"

He turned his mind back to business. "It's not a problem."

"I don't want a lawsuit tripping us up."

"Don't worry. It won't get that far." He'd make sure of that.

The investor nodded and smiled again at Amanda. "Tomorrow, then." He stepped outside.

"Good night," Amanda called, and he closed the door.

For a minute, neither moved. Luke's eyes settled on hers. Ticks from the nearby grandfather clock rent the air. It seemed strangely intimate standing together like this, as if they really were a married couple, alone in their home at last.

His gaze swept her face. The hall light grazed the curves of her cheeks, showing the deep smudges under her eyes. "I meant what I said earlier. You look tired."

"I guess I am, a little." She turned and headed to the kitchen, and he trailed her there, admiring the way her dress molded her hips.

"You did a great job. The investors liked you."

"It was fun. I told you I like to cook." She picked up a stack of plates from the table and yawned.

"Give me those." He tugged the plates from her hands. "Go sit by the pool and rest. I'll bring you a glass of wine."

"It will only take a minute to clean up."

"Amanda, you're dead on your feet." Not to mention nervous as hell—and he intended to find out why. She opened her mouth to protest, but he held his ground. "Go."

"All right. I'll just check on Claire first."

He stacked the dishes by the sink and poured the wine, then went out the patio door. She sat on the low wall near the myrtle hedge, cocooned by the malibu lights. A cool breeze had sprung up, swishing the palm trees by the pool and tousling the ends of her hair.

He handed her the glass, then sat on the wall beside her, wondering where to begin. If he asked her outright what was bothering her, she'd either deny it or claim to be tired.

"So tell me more about your project," she said.

He sipped his drink, decided to bide his time. Talking about the project might relax her, get her to open up. "What do you want to know?"

"Where are you building it?"

"Naked City. It's not actually a city," he said, when she arched a brow. "It's just an area past Sahara Avenue, outside the Strip."

The corner of her mouth edged up. "Interesting name, though."

"Yeah." He took another swallow of wine. "But that's the only interesting thing about it. It's a slum, one of the worst in Vegas. It's where I grew up."

"Really?" She looked surprised, and he didn't blame her. He never talked about his childhood, couldn't imagine why he'd mentioned it now. But there was something soothing about Amanda, something that invited confidence, trust.

"I figured you always had money," she said.

"Hardly. But the Strip was only a few blocks away. I could see it from our apartment. It might as well have been on Mars, though. It was a world apart, all that luxury and wealth." Completely out of his reach.

"So what was your family like?"

He shrugged. "Small. Poor." He frowned down at his glass. "My father split before I was born. My mother was a cocktail waitress in Harold Rothchild's casino."

The old emotions roiled through him before he could block them—bitterness, helplessness, rage. Restless, he set down his glass and walked to the hedge. Then he stood with his arms crossed and stared out at the night.

Amanda joined him a moment later. Maybe it was the quiet way she stood beside him, her shoulder brushing his arm. And maybe it was the darkness, the intimacy of the night. But suddenly, he wanted to tell her, wanted her to know.

"Her back went out," he said. "She couldn't work. She needed surgery, but we couldn't afford it."

"You didn't have insurance?"

"No. The Rothchilds blocked the unions back then, so benefits were scarce. She tried to get another job but kept missing work because of her back. And then she got hooked on pain pills. She went downhill from there."

Amanda didn't answer, but he found her silence comforting, more soothing than anything she could have said. And he realized that she understood exactly what he'd gone through. She'd also cared for her mother at an early age.

"So what did you do?" she finally asked.

"Lived on welfare. But then the rent went up and we couldn't pay. We got evicted." By their ever-compassionate slumlord, Harold Rothchild.

That moment had changed his life. He'd been twelve years old, fighting off the street gangs, scouring the garbage for food. He'd gazed at the mind-boggling luxury of the nearby Strip, the towering casino that

Rothchild owned, and he'd vowed right then that he'd be rich and powerful someday.

And that he'd avenge his mother's death.

In one more week he'd finally do it. The Phoenix would rise from the ruins of that old apartment and crush Harold Rothchild for good.

"It's not easy being poor," Amanda said gently, and he switched his attention to her. He observed her soft, wide eyes, the sympathetic set to her lips.

"No," he agreed, his voice huskier now. "It's not easy." He reached out and brushed the curve of her cheek, traced the delicate bones of her jaw. And he wondered how she had coped. She'd had a mother to support, later a kid. But she was a lot like him, a survivor. Every time life knocked her down, she'd fought back.

He ran his thumb down the bridge of her nose, over the velvety skin of her cheek. His eyes roamed her face, her curving throat, down to the tempting vee of her dress.

She was amazing, all right. Determined, protective, arousing.

"You look good in this dress." His voice deepened. "Too damned good. If Coddington hadn't stopped ogling you, I was going to slam his face into the flan."

She blinked, then let out a laugh. "Don't be silly. He wasn't ogling me."

"The hell he wasn't."

"Oh, come on. He has to be seventy years old. I probably reminded him of his granddaughter."

"He's been married five times. His current wife is twenty-one."

Her jaw dropped. "You're joking, right?"

He shook his head.

"Oh, my. You do run with a fast crowd."

"Yeah. Fast. Bad." He brushed his hand down her arm, and her smile abruptly disappeared. Sudden tension vibrated the air.

He shouldn't touch her. He was pushing the limits, testing his already strained self-control. For hours he'd been watching her smile and talk, worry and frown. He'd memorized the provocative way her lips quirked and her forehead creased, how her hair shimmered over her back. And all night long he'd been holding her, stroking her, inhaling her feminine scent as he played the part of her fiancé.

It had been four hours of exquisite torture.

And if he didn't get away from her now, he was going to break. "It's late. You'd better go inside."

"I know." Her voice came out breathless. She stayed rooted in place.

He shifted closer, drawn to the heat in her eyes, the lure of her lush, sultry lips. He stroked his hands up her arms, his blood pumping hard. Hunger built in his veins.

Kissing her would be a mistake, a complication he couldn't afford. He needed to protect her, find out why she was worried, not muddy their relationship more.

Besides, they'd agreed to keep their distance. They'd agreed this idea was bad.

But her gaze stalled on his mouth. Her breath made a provocative hitch, and the small sound tore through his nerves.

To hell with control. Ignoring her gasp, he hauled her against him. He plunged his hand in her hair, slanted his mouth over hers. And then he devoured her with a hot, urgent kiss that demolished his self-control.

He was too rough, too urgent, he knew that, but he

couldn't be gentle or nice. The whole evening had been hours of tormenting foreplay, and he was already over the edge.

She wrapped her hands around his neck and sagged against him. He inhaled the erotic heat of her skin. He gathered her closer, giving vent to his unruly hunger, and his entire body turned hard.

She moaned and wriggled against him, sending a bolt of lust to his groin. He broke the kiss, blazed a path down her velvety neck with his tongue, and his desperation surged.

He had to see her, feel her. He caught the shoulder strap of her dress in his teeth, tugged on the bow. The fabric slid down, exposing one breast. She wasn't wearing a bra.

His mind went blank. Stark need roared through his blood. She was beautiful. So damned beautiful. All ripe, perfect curves and sultry skin.

And he wanted to take her, take all of her, make her writhe and quiver and scream. He wanted to hear her breath catch, feel her heart race, make her mindless and whimpering with need.

He cupped her breast with his hand and lowered his head, loved the smooth, creamy skin with his tongue.

"Luke." She moaned and clutched his hair. Then he kissed her again, knowing he was moving too far, too fast.

But she was kissing him back, running her hands over his shoulders, his back. And he needed to feel her right where he ached.

His hands went to her bottom, and he pulled her against him, and the sweet, hot feel of her made him groan.

"Mommy?" a small voice called.

Amanda instantly stiffened. He lifted his head, lust still hazing his brain, and tightened his grip on her hips.

They couldn't stop. Not now. He was too damned aroused.

"I'm coming," she called, and tried to wriggle from his grasp. He inhaled, reluctantly let go. She jerked up her dress and retied the strap.

Her eyes were dark, her lips swollen. Her hair was a tangle of silk. He wanted to sling her over his shoulder and drag her to bed.

"I have to go," she said, sounding breathless.

"I know." But this wasn't finished, not by a long shot. And he still needed to find out what had her on edge.

He shoved his hand through his hair, made a decision. "Get your sister to babysit tomorrow. We're going hiking."

"What? Where—"

"Not far from here. I've got something to show you. And a trip will do you good."

"But…you have a meeting. I heard you talking about it tonight."

"I'm rescheduling it."

She glanced at the house, looking torn. "All right," she finally said. "If you're sure." She turned and hurried into the house.

Sure? He scoffed at that. He wasn't sure of anything right now—least of all what he'd just done. He was canceling a meeting to go hiking? Was he completely out of his mind?

He didn't know. But keeping his distance from her wasn't working. It was time for a change of plans.

Chapter 7

She was a wreck.

Amanda trudged up the trail behind Luke the next morning, so exhausted she could hardly move. All night long, she'd tossed and turned, too wound up to sleep. She'd relived every second of the thrilling evening, from Luke's heated looks to his blistering kiss. And the feel of his mouth on her breast...

She flushed, dodged a twisting juniper pine tree, then hurried to pick up her pace. She'd lectured herself for hours during the restless night, trying desperately to regain her good sense. Their engagement was fake. They had no future together. He was a billionaire play-boy, and she had a daughter to raise.

But none of that seemed to matter. All it took was the sound of his husky voice, one glance from those piercing golden eyes and she wanted to throw herself into his arms.

And if Claire hadn't interrupted them when she had…

She skidded on a patch of loose stones, and Luke whipped around and steadied her arm. "Are you all right?"

"I'm fine." Except that her heart was sprinting again. His eyes swept her body, her face, and her breath took an erratic turn. She tore her gaze away to calm her nerves.

"It's not much farther." He adjusted the pack he'd slung over his back and started walking again. She skirted a clump of cactus, knew she had to watch her step. But her eyes kept returning to the broad, strong ledge of his shoulders, his black hair gleaming in the sun. He wore loose, faded jeans—worn white in intriguing stress spots—and he looked so virile, so blatantly male that she ached to touch him again.

He stopped a moment later at a lookout point. She wiped her forehead on her sleeve, pulled her attention from his muscled biceps and looked out at the view. Directly beneath them was a small valley. A weathered wooden ranch house and derelict barn stood in the overgrown yard.

But the spot was spectacular, the views amazing. Blood-red sandstone lined the surrounding foothills. Smoky green sagebrush punctuated the rocks. The desert shimmered in the distance, topped by that startling, azure sky.

Luke glanced at her. "So what do you think?"

"It's beautiful." She inhaled the scent of juniper pines and sun-drenched earth. "How did you find this place?"

They'd driven for nearly two hours out of Vegas, most of it over teeth-jarring, washboarded roads. They'd eventually turned off the county roads onto private property and bumped along a tractor trail riddled with ruts. Then they'd hiked.

"I own it."

She blinked up at him. "This land is yours?"

He folded his muscled arms across his chest and looked out at the valley below. "I bought it about ten years ago. It's good land, a little isolated, but there's room for an airstrip near the house. There's a river and a small lake over that hill."

She glimpsed at where he was pointing, stunned. She never would have expected him to own a ranch. "What are you going to do with it?"

"Nothing, at the moment. I haven't really made any plans."

That was a relief. She'd hate to see him build a mega-resort or golf course here. She scanned the hills, absorbing the rugged, untamed beauty. The place had almost a spiritual feel.

"Did you buy it as an investment, then?"

"Not exactly." He frowned, shifted his attention back to the landscape.

Long seconds passed, so she tried again. "So why did you buy it?"

He shrugged. "It was a gift of sorts. I told you about my mother."

"Yes." She studied his profile, confused.

"She always talked about buying a ranch. You know, one of those 'when we win the jackpot' dreams. All the years I was growing up, that's all I heard about, how we were going to buy a ranch when we hit it big. So when this came on the market…"

He frowned. "It was dumb. She was already gone, and I sure as hell didn't need more land. But I don't know. It just seemed like the right thing to do."

He resumed hiking, and she followed more slowly,

her mind reeling from what he'd revealed. He'd bought this gorgeous ranch for his deceased mother. Oh, God. Emotions piled inside her, and a huge lump thickened her throat. Who would have guessed that this ruthless, powerful man had a tender side?

But she'd seen glimpses of it from the start. He'd checked on Wayne's whereabouts to ease her worries. He'd offered her the use of his house. He'd helped her when she'd blacked out, even canceled his meeting today so she could relax.

And this side of Luke scared her to death. The physical attraction was dangerous enough. But this softer side touched her heart and made her care.

And the last thing she needed now was to fall for Luke—he was a guaranteed broken heart.

But how was she going to stop?

"Be careful. This part is steep." He leaped down a small incline, then reached back and grabbed her hand. Awareness shimmered through her at the contact, and she sucked in a startled breath. Their eyes met, held. For a heartbeat, neither moved.

But then he dropped her hand and kept walking, and she struggled to regain her good sense. Maybe she was falling for Luke, but he probably just wanted sex.

And why was that so bad?

He stopped in front of a boulder. "Here it is."

Still unsettled, she glanced at the rock. An Indian petroglyph. "Oh, wow," she breathed, her turmoil abruptly forgotten. She rushed to the chunk of brown sandstone, captivated by the crudely drawn lizard etched into the rock. "I can't believe it. It's amazing."

"There are more."

"More?" She glanced around. "Where?"

He motioned ahead, and her heart skipped. Glyphs covered the surrounding boulders—etchings of deer and snakes, horses and human hands. She roamed through the rocks, entranced. "Luke, this is wonderful." To think that centuries ago, people had stood on this very spot, carving their messages into the rocks.

She studied a wavy design that might have meant water. "This probably marked a migration route or game trail." Especially since there was water nearby.

"Maybe, but there's another possibility."

Her face lifted to his. "What's that?"

"I'll show you, as long as you're not claustrophobic."

Her excitement built. "Are you saying there's a cave?"

A smile played at the edge of his mouth. "It's tight at the start, but it opens up. I'll go first with the flashlight. Just watch where you stick your hands. Rattlesnakes are active now."

Startled, she checked the ground, but not even the threat of a poisonous snake could deter her. Luke rolled aside some stones, pulled the pack off his shoulder, then squeezed through a cleft in the rocks.

She quickly followed. The opening wasn't too tight at the start, but Luke's shoulders were wider, and he had to angle them more. The air grew mustier as they entered the cave, the light dimmer. After a dozen yards, they both stooped over, then had to crawl. The walls squeezed in. There was no room to turn around. But Amanda couldn't remember when she'd enjoyed herself more.

"Almost there," Luke called back. Seconds later, the space opened up. He scrambled to his feet, still ducking, and helped her stand. "Watch your head," he cautioned. "It's low in spots." He raised the flashlight and shined it around the spacious room.

"Oh, my," she whispered, too overwhelmed to move. Primitive hunt scenes covered the walls. Hundreds of artifacts littered the ground. There were baskets, carved wooden implements, piles of arrowheads and shafts. It was incredible. She wanted to examine everything at once.

Thrilled, she twirled around.

"Easy." Luke caught her arm. She grabbed his shoulder and laughed.

"Luke, this is amazing."

"Yeah, amazing." He brushed a smudge from her cheek and angled his head. His gaze dropped to her mouth, holding her in place. And suddenly, the Indian artifacts faded away.

And then he kissed her. His mouth was warm and hard, sending waves of pleasure skidding along her nerves. And she melted into the kiss, overjoyed. This was what she'd dreamed of, longed for during that restless night.

His tongue swept her mouth. His big hand caressed her back. She moaned at the drugging sensations, the way her body pulsated with heat. She shifted closer, hoping he wouldn't stop.

But after a moment, he pulled away, then rested his forehead against hers. Her heart hammered fast. Her breath came in uneven rasps.

"Take a minute to look around, and then we'll go," he said, his voice rough.

She nodded, straightened, struggling to shift her attention back to the ruins. But she was far more interested in kissing Luke.

Still, this was the dream of a lifetime. He handed her the flashlight, and she roamed the cave, careful not to disturb anything. "Has this site been surveyed?" she asked as she examined an ancient atlatl.

"Not that I know. I've never seen it in any records. I don't think anyone knows it exists."

She skirted a stack of woven baskets, peered at a deer painted on the wall. The cave might have been a storage site, or maybe a ceremonial place, although she didn't see any remnants of fires. And it looked remarkably intact with no signs of digging or looting. The archaeologists would go berserk. "How did you find it?"

"The farmer had drawn a map. I found it with some old papers in the house."

She took another pass around the cavernous room, absorbing every detail. This was what had drawn her to archaeology—the thrill of discovery, wanting to see how ancient people had lived, wondering what they'd dreamed of, thought about and who they'd loved. The minutes passed by too fast.

"We'd better go," Luke finally said, and she reluctantly followed him from the cave. While she squinted in the blinding sunlight, he rolled the rocks into place and concealed the entrance with brush.

A short time later, they spread their picnic blanket in a patch of shade at the lookout point. Luke pulled out bottles of water and wraps.

Suddenly ravenous, she devoured her vegetable wrap, then dropped back on the blanket and sighed. She inhaled the soothing scent of sagebrush, watched a hawk ride the thermals in the sky. And for the first time in weeks, she felt relaxed, almost carefree.

"Thank you so much for showing me this, Luke. It's spectacular." To think she was one of the few people alive who'd seen it—and that Luke had realized what this would mean to her, how much she'd enjoy exploring the cave.

He stretched out beside her. "You looked tired last night, worried. I thought you could use a break." He lifted himself to one elbow, and leaned over her, kicking off a flurry of anticipation. She studied the hollows of his cheeks, the strong, masculine lines of his neck. A hint of emerging whiskers darkened his jaw.

"So what's been bothering you?" he asked. "And don't tell me it's nothing. You've been acting too jumpy for that excuse."

She sighed, knowing she could trust him, but reluctant to tell him the truth. She didn't want to reveal her mother's illness. If anyone suspected she'd inherited her mental problems, she could lose custody of Claire. And she'd die if she lost her child. Claire mattered more to her than the world.

But she also had to keep Claire safe. And if there was any chance she wasn't imagining things...

"I'm not really sure what's happening," she admitted. "It started the night I blacked out. I've been misplacing things, getting forgetful. But I really think it's just due to stress."

His eyes narrowed. "What kinds of things?"

"Small things mostly." She told him about the missing tissues and cilantro, the other bizarre events. His mouth turned hard as she talked, his eyes grim.

"And why didn't you mention this before?" His voice had a dangerous edge.

"There was no reason to. What could you do about it? You can't keep me from forgetting things."

"What if it's not you? What if someone's getting into the house? Have you thought of that?"

"Of course, I have. But you told me yourself that security system is good. And who would be getting in?

The cleaning crew hasn't been there all week. The gardeners don't come near the house. And Kendall doesn't know the code, so that just leaves me."

He leaned over her, looking predatory suddenly. "I can get in."

"And what would be your point?" She shook her head and scoffed. "You wouldn't hurt me."

His eyes bore into hers. "You're sure about that?"

The anger in his voice confused her, and she frowned. "Of course, I'm sure. You've helped me, let me stay in your house. I trust you."

His hand slid over her throat, and her heart beat fast. He looked powerful, angry...deadly. His voice dropped deeper yet. "A lot of people think I murdered Candace Rothchild."

He looked capable of murder. His eyes burned dark. His mouth was a lethal slash. Any hint of tenderness or vulnerability had disappeared.

But this was the man who'd made Claire giggle. This was the man who'd fulfilled his mother's dream, even when she wouldn't know. This was the man who made her heart race and her blood heat, who with just a kiss brought her more pleasure than she'd ever known.

This was the man she was falling for fast.

She tried to swallow. She lifted her hand to his face and traced the harsh lines framing his mouth. "You're a good man, Luke."

His eyes blazed. "The hell I am."

And then his mouth was on hers, and he was kissing her again—hot and hard and deep. She gasped at the delicious invasion, thrilled at the rough, sensual feel of his skin. The kiss was harsh, giving vent to his sudden temper, as if he wanted to prove she was wrong.

But the grinding kiss stirred her senses. She plunged her hands in his hair, roused by his delirious feel, abandoning herself to desire.

The kiss deepened, lengthened, spinning her further beyond control. She knew she should pull back, think things through, but he felt so darned good. And just once, she wanted to forget her worries, just once, she wanted to do something impulsive and surrender to the rampaging need.

He made a low, rough sound deep in his throat and shifted his weight over hers. He trailed his mouth down her neck, sending streams of pleasure rippling over her skin. She moaned.

He captured her lips again, making her head whirl. She clutched his shoulders and back. Urgency mounted inside her, and she made soft, mewling noises of need.

Then he slowed and softened the kiss, and excitement skidded through her veins. And she realized with a daze that he was an expert at this. He knew exactly when to charge and when to withdraw, how to tease and make her feel crazed. He was a connoisseur, a master of this sensual craft, and he was driving her out of her mind.

And she wanted to let him. She knew that this would change nothing. She couldn't spin this interlude into more than it was. This was sex, just sex, a brief respite from danger, a magical moment out of time.

But she needed this, wanted this. She wanted to submit to the mind-boggling pleasure, yield to the tempting bliss. All her life she'd been the responsible one, the hardworking one, the one who'd borne the weight of the world. Now, just for this moment, she wanted to forget all that—forget the fear, forget the threats, not think, not worry, just feel.

His kisses hypnotized her. The need to touch him grew frantic, overwhelming, urgent.

She gripped his shoulders and tried to pull him against her, but his mouth roamed to her throat. Then he slid his hand under her T-shirt, and his palm scorched her breast. She shuddered, growing insistent. He groaned against her throat.

He rose then and tugged off her shirt. His eyes stalled on her breasts.

Her face turned hot. She felt unprotected and exposed, even in the lacy bra. Embarrassment mingled with pleasure. His heated gaze incited her nerves.

"You're beautiful," he growled, and her breath caught. She knew it wasn't true. She wasn't gorgeous like the women he dated. And Wayne had dwelled on her shortfalls enough. But as Luke's gaze swept the length of her, she felt beautiful and desired.

Then suddenly, a gunshot shattered the silence. The sharp report thundered through the hills. Her heart froze, and she gaped at Luke. "What—"

He dove over her, mashing her into the blanket, covering her head with his chest. Her pulse scrambled. Panic seized her. Someone had shot at them, and they were out in the open, exposed.

"Behind the rocks. *Now.*" Luke rolled to his feet and yanked her upright. She scooped up her T-shirt and ran. A bullet whined past. Tension screamed through her nerves as they swerved through the scattered pines.

The edge of the cliff was littered with boulders. Luke ducked behind one, pulling her with him, and she huddled beside him and struggled to breathe. She jerked her T-shirt over her head, stuffed her arms through the sleeves, then searched for a way to escape.

The slope below them was steep and covered with sagebrush. Luke pointed to a distant cluster of pines. "Run to those trees. The trail's back there. Go straight to the car and wait. And don't stop, no matter what."

Her gaze flew to his. "But what—"

"I'm going to head him off. Now go!"

She bit her lip, reluctant to leave him. But they didn't have time to argue. The gunman could show up at any time. Luke gave her a nudge, and she leaped off the edge of the cliff.

She hit the ground and nearly fell but managed to stay on her feet. Fighting to keep her balance and control her momentum, she angled across the hill toward the trees.

She skidded in the loose dirt, plowed into some sagebrush and let out a muffled cry. But she couldn't slow, couldn't stop. She had to reach the safety of those trees.

But what was Luke doing? Had their attacker seen him? How could he stop a man with a gun?

Then another shot rang out. She zigzagged in alarm.

She reached the pine trees and whipped behind one, then whirled around to look. The hillside was empty. Luke was nowhere in sight. Where on earth had he gone?

And where was the gunman? *Who* was the gunman? Why had he been shooting at them?

She hauled in a ragged breath, forcing those thoughts from her mind. She'd worry about all that later. She had to get to the car and wait for Luke.

But the path wound below her across the open slope, visible from above. She hesitated, still struggling to catch her breath. What if the gunman had her in his sights?

She fought back a spurt of dread, trying to decide

what to do. Luke had told her not to stop. He was buying her time to reach the car. But then how was he going to get down?

Another shot barked out. Sheer panic bludgeoned her nerves. What if Luke had been hit?

She couldn't leave him. She had to go back and check. But both the hillside and trail were too exposed. She had to find another way up.

The only other route was over the rocks. She darted to the nearby boulders, scrambled through the silvery sage. A chuckwalla scurried past, and she bit back a startled shriek.

Calm down, she told herself firmly. The lizard wouldn't hurt her. She climbed over some rocks, eased around a yucca plant, then eyed the long stretch of sandstone above.

She had no choice. She had to climb it. At least it wasn't too steep, and there were bushes and ridges to grip. As long as she went slowly, she would be fine.

She clambered up, then crept across the rock face, the hot sun scorching her scalp. Her heart beat fast. Sweat beaded and trickled down her jaw. She grabbed a plant, boosted herself up, then reached for a nearby ledge.

An ominous rattle stopped her. Unable to move, she jerked her gaze to the side.

A rattlesnake hissed at her, preparing to strike.

Chapter 8

The wild scream shattered the silence, sending adrenaline streaming through Luke's blood. *Amanda.* She was in danger. He had to get to her fast. But he couldn't move yet, not with the shooter just a few yards away. Even the soft snap of a twig could tip him off.

He sucked air through his tightly clenched teeth and crushed back the mushrooming fear. He had to stay calm, think through the haze of panic, stay smart or he'd get them both killed.

Insects buzzed in the bushes around him. A turkey vulture soared overhead. Blood dripped down his left arm from where the bullet had grazed him, and his shoulder hammered with pain. He adjusted the handkerchief he'd knotted as a makeshift bandage, shifted his gaze to the bushes ahead.

Concentrate. Be patient. The man who stayed focused was the one who survived. He'd learned that lesson on Las Vegas's deadly streets.

He just wished he had a handgun or knife.

The bushes rustled, and his vision tunneled. His body shook with the need to attack.

His pursuer rose, crept into the open with his pistol drawn. Then he turned in the direction of Amanda's scream.

Big mistake.

Luke leaped out, slammed into his side. They hit the ground grunting and rolled.

Luke landed on top. The man twisted, thrust back his elbow. Luke took the jab to his chest. He groaned, shook off the pain and fought for an opening, landed a punch to the man's gut.

The man wheezed and quickly recovered, then raised his pistol to shoot. But Luke lunged, tackled him again, scrambling for an advantage in the thick cloud of dust. He grabbed the man's wrist and rammed it against the ground.

His muscles strained as he battled to hold him. Sweat burned into his eyes. He grappled for dominance, straining and shoving, until the man's hand finally went slack. The pistol skidded loose.

But the man butted his head into Luke's injured shoulder. Luke went dizzy with the fierce waves of pain. *Damn.*

He hauled back, slammed his fist into his attacker's head and the sickening thump vibrated through his arm. The man slumped against the ground and went still.

Luke wheezed in the dusty air, shook the stinging sweat from his eyes. He pushed himself up, his muscles trembling from the adrenaline dump. Then he staggered over and picked up the gun.

A 9mm Glock. He released the magazine to count the rounds, slammed it back home and racked the slide. Feeling less vulnerable now, he stuffed it into the waistband of his jeans.

But he couldn't go to Amanda yet. He strode back to his attacker and kicked him over, then lowered himself to one knee. He rifled through the man's pockets but came up empty. No identification, not even a damned set of keys. He took a long look at his face— Hispanic, swarthy complexion, high cheekbones. Late thirties, early forties, judging by the receding hair.

He scowled. Too bad he'd left his cell phone in the car. He could have photographed this thug.

Frustrated, he exhaled and glanced around. He didn't have a rope to restrain him, and he couldn't waste any more time. He'd have to leave him, hope the police picked him up later on.

His urgency mounting, he leaped up and ran down the trail, the memory of that scream echoing through his mind. He shouldn't have left her alone. What if she'd been captured or worse? He immediately pushed aside that awful thought, needing to focus on finding her fast.

At the top of a hill he paused and scanned the landscape, searching for movement, or anything out of place. The sun sizzled off the blood-red sandstone. A hawk passed by, dragging a shadow over the earth.

Then a speck of blue in the sagebrush snagged his attention, and his heart careened to a stop. She'd been wearing a blue T-shirt and jeans.

His gut balled tight now, he raced across the parched hillside, hurdling creosote bushes and rocks. Had she been shot? He hadn't heard another gun fire. But then why had she veered off the trail?

He reached her seconds later. She lay facedown in the dirt surrounded by yucca plants and sagebrush. He dropped to his knees, leaned close to check her pulse. "Amanda. Amanda."

"Luke." She groaned, lifted her head.

She was alive. Thank God. He sagged, closed his eyes and exhaled, his own pulse running amok. He snapped his eyes open again. "What happened?"

She propped herself on her elbows and hung her head. "There was a snake."

Oh, hell. "Where did he get you?" he demanded, running his hands over her back.

"He didn't. I fell down the rocks. I hit some cactus, and my ankle…"

She'd fallen? He scowled up at the wall of sandstone. "What were you doing up there?"

"I heard that gunshot. I thought you might have been hurt. I was trying to go back to see."

His jaw turned slack. He stared at her in disbelief. "So you tried to climb the cliff?"

She didn't answer, and he bit back a curse, his fear for her out of control. But he'd have it out with her later. He needed to get her to safety first.

With effort he held on to his temper and managed to gentle his voice. "Where did you hit the cactus?"

"The back of my leg." She groaned again. "My right thigh."

He scooted closer, wincing when he spotted a dozen thick spines embedded in her jeans. No way could she ride in the car like that. Taking off her pants might jar the spines loose—or twist them and torture her more.

"I'll have to pull them out," he told her. He rose,

quartered the area for sticks, finally found two the right size. "This is going to hurt like hell, though."

He knelt beside her again, caught hold of a spine with the sticks. "Brace yourself." He jerked it from her thigh, flicked it away. She bit off an anguished cry.

He grimaced, sorry to be causing her more pain, but he didn't have much choice. Working as fast as he could, he pulled out the spines and tossed them a safe distance away. Then he ran his hand carefully over her thigh. "I think that's it. We'll check you out better when we get back."

"Thanks."

He shook his head. She hardly owed him thanks. His big attempt to help her relax today had only made things worse.

"Here. Hold on to me," he said as she struggled to rise. He grabbed her waist, slung her arm over his shoulder and helped her to her feet.

She took a step, nearly collapsed. "My ankle." She tried again and gasped. "I think I sprained it."

"Lean on me more." He helped her adjust her grip, glanced at her dirt-streaked face. She looked a wreck— her long hair wild, one cheek bleeding, her blue eyes shimmering with tears. But despite the grime—despite her pain—her soft, natural beauty wound through him, touching his heart.

He'd never had anyone try to save him before. He lived in a high-stakes, cutthroat world—a world where money ruled, the strong survived and every man looked out for himself. It was a world he understood, a world he'd mastered. He'd clawed his way to the top, stopping for no one, and now he was the one with the power.

Or he would be, once that project went through.

But Amanda was different. She was loyal, gentle, protective—even of him.

And that thought disturbed him. It brought back memories of his childhood, the way he'd once been before reality had smacked him down, feelings he'd buried for years. Because gentleness weakened a man. It left him vulnerable, ripe for attack.

"Luke, you're bleeding."

Still unsettled, he shook his head. "It's just a graze. I'll take care of it when we get back to town."

She gnawed her lip, glanced around. "Where's the gunman?"

"Still up there. I knocked him out and took his gun." And hopefully, gained them some time.

But he couldn't afford to take chances. As they worked their way to the car, their breaths rasping in the quiet air, he focused again on the hills. They'd had a close call, too close, and he wouldn't be caught off guard again.

A few minutes later, they reached his Land Rover, only to find that the tires had been slashed.

"Oh, no." Amanda turned to him. "What are we going to do now?"

"We don't have much choice. We'll drive on the rims, at least until we can pick up a cell phone signal and call for a tow."

He helped her into her seat, climbed into the driver's side. Despite his denial, his left arm throbbed. It was going to be a long ride back for them both.

Ignoring the pain, he cranked the engine, relieved when it started up. He drove along the rutted tractor trail, jolted through a dried-out creek bed. The ruined tires slapped against the dirt.

The slashed tires bothered him. It felt personal, more

like an act of rage than an attempt to strand them—especially since the engine had been left alone.

He looked at Amanda. "What does your ex look like?"

"Wayne? He's about five ten, blond, a heavy build. Why? Was it him back there?"

"No. This guy looked Hispanic, maybe part Indian."

"Oh. I'd hoped…" She turned her gaze to the windshield and hugged her arms.

"What?"

"Nothing."

"Have you seen him before?"

She frowned, shook her head. "I don't think so. The guy who tried to kidnap Claire was wearing a ski mask, so I didn't see his face. I didn't see the man in your casino, either."

He swerved to avoid a hole. "I saw the surveillance tape. His hair was longer than this guy's, and lighter brown. It wasn't him."

She looked at him again. "The waiter the other night… He might have been Hispanic."

That didn't mean much. Half the western population had Hispanic roots. But if this was the same man, it meant Harold Rothchild had hired this guy. But then where did the casino gunman come in?

He scowled. Damn, this was complicated. And another thing bothered him—how had their attacker found them today? Few people knew he owned this land, and he hadn't announced his plans. Unless the gunman had been watching and then followed them here. He could have hung back, followed their dust trail. Without a breeze to disperse it, they'd probably raised dust for at least five miles.

He was still mulling that over when he reached the

barbed wire gate at the end of the tractor path. He idled the engine and hopped out. But as he dragged the gate open, he spotted a Jeep by the trees down the road.

His spirits rising, he jogged back and turned off the engine, then grabbed his cell phone and keys. "We found a replacement car. Come on."

"But how are you going to drive it without a key?" She opened her door, and he helped her out.

"Don't worry." He'd picked up more than just survival skills on the streets.

And this job turned out to be easy. The dashboard had already been torn apart, the wires exposed. "It looks like he stole it." No point searching the vehicle for clues about his identity, then.

He touched the wires and started the engine. "Ready?" She nodded, and he drove off. They hit a bump, and she moaned.

He kept his attention on the sun-baked road, trying to avoid the worst of the washboard and ruts. But as he drove toward the highway, a cloud of dust billowing in his wake, the memory of Amanda's scream shuddered through him, that god-awful moment when he'd feared that she could be dead.

This situation had grown more dangerous today. This wasn't just about the ring anymore, or even an ex-husband bent on revenge. Someone had tried to kill them. Someone had followed them into the hills and hunted them down. They'd only survived due to luck.

But Luke knew better than to trust in luck. He'd built his fortune on the harsh reality that luck didn't last, that every gambler eventually lost.

So how could he keep Amanda safe? She wouldn't leave town; he'd already tried that tack.

He glanced sideways, took in her dusty clothes and tousled hair, the way her full lips flattened with pain. And he realized he didn't have a choice. He had to stay close to protect her. This had gone beyond lust, beyond mutual favors, two people helping each other out. Amanda's life was at stake.

And from now on—whether she liked it or not—he wasn't letting her out of his sight.

Amanda stared out Luke's penthouse window later that night, watching the city lights glitter against the sky. She'd gone from extreme highs to terrible lows today, from the ecstasy of nearly making love to Luke to barely escaping death.

But at whose hands? Certainly not Wayne's—which was terrible news. Not that she wanted Wayne after her. But at least he was a known enemy, one who she could fight. And it would have explained the bizarre events in the house. Wayne was vindictive, controlling. It would be just like him to try to mess with her mind.

But that hadn't been Wayne on that hill.

Her stomach in turmoil, she adjusted her grip on her crutches and hobbled back to the couch. She sank into the soft, creamy leather, propped her bandaged ankle on the ottoman and closed her eyes.

What a disaster moving here had been. Her life had spun completely out of control. She'd escaped an abusive ex-husband only to land in an even worse mess.

And to top it off, she'd discovered that she might have inherited her mother's mental illness.

But she couldn't wallow in self-pity or dwell on her fears. She had Claire to keep safe. She exhaled again, trying to purge the anxiety from her voice, then punched in Kendall's number on her phone.

"It's about time," Kendall complained when she picked up. "Where are you?"

"Luke's penthouse."

"How's your ankle?"

"Just sprained." She'd phoned Kendall earlier from the urgent care clinic to update her on the news. "But I'm staying here tonight."

Silence greeted that statement. "It's not what you think," she added. Although it nearly had been back in the hills.

"Mandy…"

"You don't have to say it. I know."

"But you don't even know this guy." Amanda opened her mouth to argue, but her sister forged on. "I know he's rich, and I know he's letting you stay here, which is nice. But for God's sake, Mandy, get real. Luke Montgomery isn't your type."

Her temper stirred. The last thing she needed after her hellish day was a lecture from her sister about men. "So who is my type? Wayne?"

"Don't be ridiculous. You know I never liked that creep. But that's the problem. Luke might be just as bad."

"He's not—"

"It was all over the news today. He had a restraining order on Candace Rothchild."

Amanda's temper abruptly deflated. *A restraining order.* Her belly churned even more. She glanced over her shoulder at the hall to Luke's bedroom and lowered her voice. "That doesn't make him a killer."

"But you don't know what might have happened

that night. They argued in his casino—everyone saw it. And maybe she provoked him later on. Maybe he flew into a rage."

Amanda shuddered and rotated her wrist, remembering Wayne. But Luke wasn't like that. Yes, he was a hard man, a powerful one. But he'd saved her life today. He'd taken a bullet to keep her safe.

She shoved her hand through her freshly washed hair and sighed. "Listen, you don't have to worry about me. I know what I'm doing."

"Do you?" Kendall's voice went flat. "Look, I know I'm always after you to take more chances, but not this one."

"Don't worry. I'll be fine." She hoped. Gathering her courage, she fiddled with the tie on the thick, fluffy bathrobe from the spa downstairs. She dreaded asking but needed to know. "You're all right, aren't you? I mean, nothing strange has happened at the house today?"

"No, why?" Suspicion tinged Kendall's voice. "Is there something I need to know?"

"No." She closed her eyes, pressed her fingers to her temple. There went her last remaining long shot—that someone was targeting the house. "I just wanted to make sure you were both all right."

"We're fine. We've been swimming, coloring, reading books… Hold on." There was a muffled commotion in the background. "Here's Claire now."

"Hi, Mommy." Claire's voice chirped over the line. She babbled about Aunt Kendall and Brownie, the minutia of the day's events.

Amanda's throat turned thick as she listened. It would kill her to lose custody of Claire. But if she did have her mother's illness, she couldn't endanger her child. She had to do everything she could to keep her safe, even if it meant giving her up.

And she knew exactly how the illness would progress—the paranoia and delusions, the tormenting voices and suicidal thoughts. Not one medication on the market had helped her mother cope.

She beat back that frightening thought, then forced a peppy note into her voice so she wouldn't scare Claire. "Be good for Aunt Kendall tonight. And eat all your oatmeal in the morning."

Her chest aching, her throat so tight she could hardly speak, she told Claire she loved her and clicked off the phone. Then she closed her eyes, sagged back against the cushions and tried to think.

All right. So she might have inherited her mother's illness. The thought terrified her, but it was a possibility she had to face. She'd have to see a doctor for an evaluation, make contingency plans for Claire. But not yet. She still had time before her behavior got too erratic—assuming she really was ill. She'd take this day by day.

And she wouldn't just sit around pitying herself in the meantime. She was stronger than that.

Agitated, needing to do something, anything to take her mind off the fear, she grabbed her crutches and rose. She hobbled into the spotless kitchen and cleared away the remnants of the five-star dinner room service had brought.

Then, her emotions still all over the map, she dimmed the lights and started toward the guest suite to crash. Things always looked better in the morning, her mother had said. But nothing had improved for her mother. And somehow, she didn't see how a few more hours would remedy this mess.

Partway down the hall, she remembered Luke. She paused, wondering if she should check on him before she turned in. He might be having second thoughts about that pain medication he'd refused. Not that she blamed him for being leery given his mother's addiction. But at least she could ask.

She returned to the kitchen and grabbed the pills, then worked her way down his hall. Seconds later, she tapped on his bedroom door. "Luke?" He didn't answer, so she inched the door open and called again. "Luke?"

Still no answer. She went inside and scanned the enormous room. The overhead light was still on, and her gaze zeroed in on the bed. Luke lay face down on the oversized mattress, his arms stretched out, his face turned to the side. His upper body was naked, his lower half covered by sheets. Despite his claim that he'd had work to do, he'd apparently fallen asleep.

She put the pain pills on the bedside table with the antibiotics, poured water from a nearby carafe. Then she hesitated, debating whether to wake him. He needed another antibiotic soon.

Her pulse quickening, she set down her crutches and perched on the edge of the mattress. For a long moment, she indulged herself, letting her eyes travel over his back. His skin was tanned, smooth, the muscles of his broad back clearly defined. Her gaze lingered on his massive shoulders, the strong, rugged lines of his neck. His upper arm was bandaged where the bullet had grazed him, and the cloth gleamed white against his skin.

She touched his arm to check for infection, relieved that his skin wasn't hot. She knew she should wake him, then leave. She couldn't just sit here forever and stare.

But his face held her riveted—the dark, aggressive brows, the black whiskers coating his jaw. He had a strong, masculine nose, thick, ink-black hair, the most intriguing, sensual mouth. Her mind stalled on the memory of how he'd kissed her, and shivers rippled over her skin.

Even asleep he looked virile and dangerous. She'd never seen anyone so powerfully male.

No wonder women found him compelling. He had enormous wealth, the kind of good looks that drew women of every age. And that intensity in his eyes...

But how many women saw the caring part? How many knew about that land? How many glimpsed his complexity or sensed the pain that drove this man?

She snorted at that wild thought. She hardly knew him, either. Her sister was right about that. She'd only met Luke last week.

And as much as she hated to admit it, Kendall was right about something else. She probably shouldn't trust him. She'd made that mistake with Wayne. Marrying Wayne had been the one time she'd taken a chance, the one time she'd let impulse and wishful thinking override common sense. And that had been a disaster.

But if getting close to Luke was wrong, then why did he feel so right?

His eyes opened. He turned his head, and those golden eyes fastened on hers.

And suddenly the air turned too thick to breathe.

"I was dreaming about you," he said, his voice deep, husky.

Her throat went dry. She couldn't move. And she was suddenly, intensely aware of how close he lay, how naked she was beneath her robe.

And a torrent of erotic memories whipped through her—the heat of his mouth, the musk of his skin, the exciting caress of his hands.

His eyes darkened, holding her captive. Warmth pooled between her thighs. He'd dreamed of her, wanted her.

She hungered for him just as badly. She ached to relive that sensual pleasure, find out where it could lead. She wanted to abandon herself to this delirious attraction—forget the danger, forget her worries, forget the horrific time bomb ticking in her head.

He reached up, snagged the back of her neck with his hand and drew her close.

"Luke," she whispered, her voice raw. "Make me forget."

His eyes turned hotter yet. He tugged her closer until her mouth was inches from his.

He lowered his gaze to her lips, brushed the bottom curve with his thumb, making shivers dance over her skin.

"That's the hell of it." His voice came out rough, almost angry.

"What?" she whispered, too muddled with desire to think.

"I don't want you to forget. I want you to remember. *Remember me.*"

His mouth took hers. She would remember him, all right. How could she help it?

This was the man she was starting to love.

Chapter 9

She was heaven, absolute, erotic bliss.

Luke pulled Amanda against him, his mouth capturing hers in a hot, deep kiss that demolished his self-control. His tongue dueled with hers. Raw heat thickened his blood. He plunged his hand through her silky hair, felt her soft, full breasts pillow his chest, and the perfect, sensual feel of her shut down his mind.

He'd been fantasizing about her for days now—how she'd look naked, her moist heat pulsing around him, those endlessly riveting legs hooked over his back. Kissing her hadn't been nearly enough, had only fired his imagination more.

But even the most vivid dream couldn't match the reality of Amanda. The scent of her slick, creamy skin, the sweep of her satin hair over his chest drew a ragged groan from his throat. He dragged her further over his body, ran his hands up her legs beneath the robe, stroking the velvety sweep of her thighs.

She was so soft, so lush, so damned arousing. The way she yielded to him, melting around him, those provocative moans she made in the back of her throat.

But suddenly she flinched, gasped against his mouth. He broke the kiss, alarmed. "What's wrong?"

"My ankle." She winced, closed her eyes on a shudder of pain.

He silently swore. He'd forgotten her sprained ankle. "Let's change places." He tipped her gently onto her back, slipped a pillow under her foot so he wouldn't bump it again. Then, ignoring his own throbbing arm, he braced himself on his elbows above her.

Her gaze dropped to his bandaged bicep. "Your arm—"

"Doesn't hurt." Not nearly as much as another, painfully engorged part of him did.

But doubt clouded her eyes. She nibbled her bottom lip, her frown deepening, and he tried to beat back the lust.

"Having second thoughts?"

"No, not exactly, it's just…I have to tell you…" Her face turned pink, and her gaze flitted away. "You might not want… I'm not too good at this."

He would have laughed if she hadn't looked so distressed. Not good at this? He was so hot for her he was ready to explode. "What makes you think that?"

"My ex-husband. He said I wasn't…" Her blush deepened, and she fidgeted with the collar on her robe.

He went still. "He said you weren't what?"

"That I wasn't…exciting enough. That he needed to, you know…" Her face flaming, her eyes stayed on her robe. "Watch videos, or look at magazines to get…" Her voice trailed off.

He closed his eyes on a flash of anger, damning Wheeler for all the damage he'd done. Then he tilted up her delicate chin, let his gaze rove her sultry lips.

Her blue eyes were dark with lust. Her tousled hair cascaded around her face. He ached to fist his hands in that glorious hair, kiss the fragile sweep of her throat, explore every rapturous inch of her skin.

Keeping his eyes locked on hers, he trapped her hand and slowly, relentlessly pushed it over his chest and past his belly until she cupped him, cupped all of him, every rock-hard, throbbing inch.

Her eyes widened. Her lips parted on a soundless gasp. He pulsed against her, heavy, thick, ready to erupt.

"I think," he said gruffly, "we can safely say the problem wasn't you."

"No." Her voice sounded strangled. "Not me."

He nipped her lips, parting them with his tongue. And then he drove his tongue in deeply, letting her feel the violent need rocking his blood.

She whimpered in response, wrapped her arms around his neck, bringing her soft body tighter against his. Hunger rippled through him, the relentless beat bludgeoning him like shock waves from a nuclear blast. But he had to go slowly. He wanted to drive her to ecstasy, shatter every illusion she had about her lack of appeal, obliterate every single memory of Wheeler from her mind.

And make her remember *him*.

He forced himself to ease off, even as his body shuddered with need. He slowed and lengthened the kiss, caressed her with long, languid strokes. He slid his hands down her lush, smooth curves, seducing, teasing, arousing. She arched against him, her excitement growing, and he swallowed her moan with his lips.

Unable to resist, he grazed her jaw, her neck, then worked his way down her body, replacing his hand with his mouth. Her nipples pouted in invitation, then pebbled at his heated response. He smiled when she groaned and tugged his hair.

"You're so damned beautiful," he murmured. And her ex-husband was a fool.

He stroked her belly, her thighs, feathering kisses up her sensitive skin until she was shaking with need. He teased, circled, retreated, beating back his own burgeoning hunger, wanting to make this a night she would never forget.

But the restraint was taking its toll. His heart thundering now, his breath growing ragged and fast, he moved back up her body and took her mouth. He plundered deeply, moving over her, letting her feel his insistent need.

But he wanted to make her feel just as desperate, just as crazed. He raised himself up and looked at her—her parted lips, her sultry eyes, the silky tendrils of hair clinging to her flushed cheeks. She was open to him, her entire body exposed, looking like every dream he'd ever had.

He ran his palms down her breasts to her taut belly, back over her satiny thighs. His muscles bunched, and he struggled to keep his own raw needs in check. But she arched her back, and the movement sent a heavy jolt of hunger through his veins. She was torturing him, and he was fast veering out of control.

He poised his body over hers. "Open your eyes." His throat was thick, his voice hoarse. Her dazed gaze rose to his. He trembled, his control eroding, wanting desperately to plunge into that tempting heat.

"Luke," she whispered. "Do something." Her hands gripped his shoulders, his back, and she tried to tug him against her.

He framed her face with his hands, using every ounce of willpower he had to keep from taking her fast. He entered her as slowly as he could, giving her time to accommodate him, to adjust, but the hot, sensual feel of her incinerated his nerves.

When he'd sheathed himself completely, he closed his eyes and rested his forehead against hers, trying to breathe through the rampaging need. He throbbed insistently inside her, his body clamoring to move. But he had to slow down, make this right for her, erase the pain from her past.

He opened his eyes, ran his finger over her cheek. He looked into her eyes, wanting to reassure her, but those mesmerizing blue eyes held him enthralled.

Emotions poured through him, disturbing emotions. Emotions he didn't dare name.

This was sex. That's all this was—a night of sex, nothing more.

He kissed her again, his urgency soaring, his body lost to the need. She closed around him, warm and wet and tight. And his hunger intensified, riding him like a whip, a mandate he couldn't ignore.

He let his body find the primitive rhythm, fulfilling that most basic need. That's all this was, he assured himself through the blaze of heat. Just biology, a man and woman indulging in natural urges, nothing more.

It couldn't be more.

His heart thudded fast. The slow pace made him

crazed. Nothing had felt this urgent, this right in his entire life.

His desperation built. Desire clawed at him, threatening to pull him under. He slid his hand down her body between them, then stroked her most sensitive flesh.

She shuddered and bucked against him. "Luke," she cried. But she was holding back, fighting her release, her nails biting into his shoulders and arms.

But this was a war he intended to win. He gripped her chin, forcing her dazed eyes to his. Willing her to surrender to the pleasure. Submit. "Let go," he ordered.

Her eyes pleaded with his. "I can't. I—"

"Do it. Let go *now.*"

She stiffened, came undone with a keening cry. His satisfaction soared. He felt like a conqueror for giving this woman what Wheeler never had.

He gripped her jaw and kissed her, a deep, wild kiss that showed her exactly how ravenous he was. And then he gave in to the need, let his instincts take charge. The pressure built, his body quickening beyond his control. And he exploded into her, his hoarse cry joining hers.

But as he drifted back to earth long moments later, he wondered what the hell he'd just done.

When Luke lifted his head from the pillow hours later, Amanda was gone. He blinked, his vision blurry from lack of sleep, and pondered the now-empty bed. But it was hard to hold on to a thought with pleasure still hazing his brain. It had been one hell of a night. They'd made love until dawn, then finally succumbed to exhaustion and dozed.

The sex had been phenomenal. Amanda had fascinated him with her surprising demands. She'd blasted past her inhibitions, demolishing her preconceptions, proving that her body was made for hot sex.

Made for him.

His own body was sated, depleted. He inhaled the scent of sex on the rumbled sheets, closed his eyes on a groan. Erotic images of the night flashed past, and his body predictably throbbed.

Maybe not so depleted.

And where was she, anyhow? He sat up, scrubbed his hand over his bristly jaw and rubbed his gritty eyes. And his mind danced around the other memories, the emotions that had surfaced during the night. But he pushed those confusing feelings aside. He'd analyze his reaction to her later.

He got out of bed, ignoring the burn in his injured arm, the insistent arousal her lingering scent caused. He pulled on a pair of loose sweatpants, padded barefoot down the carpeted hallway to the front room.

She stood in front of the floor-to-ceiling windows that comprised one wall, staring out at the early morning sky. Her arms were crossed, her shoulders hunched as if she was cold. The wave of possessiveness he felt caught him off guard.

But her eyes met his in the reflection, and something about her expression made him pause.

"Morning-after regrets?"

"I think you know better than that." Her voice turned soft, and he knew she was remembering exactly how much she'd enjoyed the night. "I just couldn't sleep."

It had been spectacular, all right. He walked to her, slid his arms around her waist from behind, and the feel of her warm, soft bottom stoked his desire. He savored the scent of her hair, slid his hands down her belly and thighs.

Her eyes locked on his in the glass. "Again?"

He grunted. He could spend days, months exploring every facet of this woman. But sex could wait. He didn't like that worried look in her eyes.

"So how come you're not sleeping?"

She sighed, and the soft sound twisted his heart. "I just had a bad dream, that's all."

"About your ex?"

"Wayne...the gunman. Everything that's been happening in the past couple weeks. I came out here to read so I wouldn't bother you."

Her lips wobbled, and even in the reflection he could see the fatigue darkening her skin beneath her eyes. He frowned. He hadn't helped much by keeping her up all night.

But maybe he could ease some of her cares. "I didn't have a chance to tell you, but I put in a phone call to Natalie Rothchild last night when we got back. They did a parole compliance check on your ex. He's still in Maryland."

"That's good." But she didn't look relieved. If anything, the fear in her eyes intensified. And he suspected that something else was bothering her, something more than the obvious danger. She'd had the same scared look back at the house.

And he still intended to discover the cause.

"Do you really think Harold Rothchild is behind all this?" she asked.

"It makes the most sense." He released her, walked to the window, braced his forearm on the glass and peered out. The darkness was fading, giving way to the dawn. It would soon be another scorching day under the desert sun.

"His business has been in trouble for years," he added. "He's taken out some high-interest loans that are coming due, and he won't make the payments." Loans from the mob-connected Schaffers. "I've timed it so the Phoenix will take away business at a critical time. He'll have to start selling assets soon. Once that happens, his entire empire will collapse." He couldn't keep the satisfaction from his voice.

"You're saying you planned this? You're doing this on purpose to make him fail?" She sounded appalled.

He swung back to her and met her gaze. "Don't pity him, Amanda. He's ruined enough lives in his time. He deserves far worse than this." The man's indifference had killed his mother, causing her addiction and early demise.

"I see." She let out a short laugh. "And you really think he'd try to kill us to stop this project?"

"He'll do anything to hold on to his power. This is a high-stakes game. No one plays nice, not even me."

Her voice turned low. "But you'd never kill anyone."

"No." But he'd done other things he wasn't proud of, things he'd had to do to win.

She hobbled to the window and looked out. For a long moment she didn't speak, just stared out at the pink sky streaking the horizon beyond the black peaks. "So where is Naked City?" she asked at last.

"Over there." He pointed out a darkened area just past the lighted Strip.

"So you can see your old neighborhood from here."

"Yeah. I can see it from here." It served as a reminder of where he'd come from, kept him focused on his goals. And before long he'd stand right here and watch bulldozers raze that slum.

She gave him a worried glance. "I hope canceling the meeting yesterday didn't cause any problems."

He shrugged. In truth, it had ticked off the investors. He'd spent hours the other night making phone calls, trying to make amends, which had been harder than he'd thought. Canceling that meeting had been a stupid move, foolhardy. This project was too damned important—everything he'd worked toward for twenty years. He couldn't afford to take risks now.

"Do you have a picture of it?" she asked.

"The project? Yeah, on the desk." He strode back to the sofa, got her crutches and handed them to her. Then he crossed the room to the desk.

He flicked on the desk lamp, spread out the rolled-up plans, and secured the corners with weights. She joined him a moment later.

She stood close enough beside him that their shoulders touched, and he inhaled her sensual scent. His eyes roamed her tousled hair, the tempting cleavage exposed by the gaping robe.

He wondered why he wasn't tired of her by now. Usually one night with a woman stifled his curiosity, leaving him bored. Hell, half the time he couldn't wait for the woman to leave.

But Amanda was different. Instead of wanting her out of his penthouse so he could get back to work, he couldn't draw his gaze from her lips.

"So what do you think?" he asked, oddly anxious to hear her opinion.

She pursed her lips, ran her finger over the architectural drawing, slanted her head to see the painted images along the sides. "It's fabulous." She shook her head, and her hair slid over her shoulders, glimmering as it caught the light. "It's a magnificent project, huge, like the ancient pyramids."

His mouth quirked up. "It's not that great." But her words sent warmth flowing through him. He was glad she liked it, that she approved.

He shifted his gaze to the painting of the mythical bird at the top of the plans. The Phoenix, the mighty, fabled bird, able to regenerate and recover from death. Crimson and gold, it would perch atop the casino—proud, regal, triumphant.

Just like him. Harold Rothchild had treated his mother like trash, like someone disposable, someone whose life didn't matter to him. He'd crushed her, assuming that an impoverished nobody could never battle his power and wealth. He'd been right.

But he hadn't reckoned on Luke.

Amanda's eyes returned to his. "I read an article about the project in the paper while you were sleeping." She hesitated, and another small line furrowed her brow. "It said people have been protesting this project, that they want affordable housing built there instead."

He shrugged, rolled up the plans and set them aside. "That's normal. There are always protests with a project this size."

Her troubled gaze stayed on his. "But what about the people who live in those apartments? Where are they going to go?"

"They'll find another place."

"Are you sure?"

"Yeah, I'm sure. It's not a problem." But his growing desire for her was. And suddenly, he didn't want to think about the project anymore, not with this warm, willing woman standing there naked beneath that robe.

He moved close, crowding her against the desk. The scent of her skin filled his nostrils and fired his blood. He slid his hand around her neck, studied the pale freckles sprinkling the bridge of her nose. "You worry too much."

Her mouth tightened. "I can't help it. There's a lot to worry about right now."

He couldn't deny that. She'd been shot at, held up at gunpoint, possibly drugged. Someone had even tried to steal her child. And she didn't deserve any of this. She was just an innocent victim, caught in the crossfire of his revenge.

"I'm going to keep you safe," he promised. From whatever threatened her. "I won't let anything happen to you."

"I know." She gave him a tremulous smile.

Her confidence floored him. And those emotions bubbled to the surface again, the desire to protect her, defend her, to claim her as his.

"I meant what I said yesterday," she whispered. "You're a good man, Luke."

"Not that good." Not much better than Rothchild in some respects. "Don't make me into something I'm not."

She slowly shook her head. "You're better than you think."

The hell he was. His anger flared—anger at himself for his ruthless past, anger at her for her misguided trust. He didn't want her looking at him as if he were a hero. He wanted her to see him, see who he really was.

He took the crutches from her hands and tossed them to the carpet, his gaze never wavering from hers. Then he lifted her onto the desk and stepped between her legs.

Right where he wanted to stay.

His hands went to the belt on her robe, and he made short work of the tie. He jerked the robe open and ripped it off. And then he let his gaze slowly rake every provocative, naked inch of her, from her sweetly curving breasts to the heaven at the juncture of her thighs.

His gaze lingered, traveled back up and her already-dazed eyes locked on his. Her lush lips parted. Her breath came in reedy gasps.

And that now-familiar hunger blazed through his blood.

"This isn't going to be nice or slow," he warned her. "I'm going to take you fast and hard."

Shock and excitement flared in her eyes. "I don't want nice or slow. I want you." She raised her hands to his shoulders. Her eyes stayed riveted on his.

Her trust made him even angrier. He slipped himself free of his sweatpants, lifted her bottom and in one, swift motion drove himself home.

They both groaned. But he'd told her the truth. And this time, he didn't play the cultured billionaire, didn't pretend to be nice. He took her hard and rough, treating her with brutal honesty, letting her feel the man he was.

A man raised in the gutter. The illegitimate son of a drifter. In a few hard thrusts, she convulsed.

He joined her barely a second later. Delirium deluged his blood. He was still pulsing inside her when a soft ring sounded across the room.

"That's my cell phone," she said, sounding distracted. "I'd better get it."

"Yeah." And suddenly, since the first time he'd touched her the night before, he needed distance. He didn't know what had just happened, but it scared the hell out of him.

Glad for the interruption, he quickly retreated. He adjusted his sweatpants, stalked across the room to get the phone. By the time he returned to the desk, she stood holding her crutches, safely enveloped in the robe.

Still shaken by what had just happened, he handed her the phone. She looked at the display and frowned, then clicked it on. "Hi. What's up?"

Her face paled. "Oh, God." She swayed, put out a hand to grasp the desk.

He tensed, kept his gaze on hers.

"I'll be right there." She snapped the phone closed, and her panic-stricken eyes met his. "It's Claire. I need to get to the hospital fast."

Chapter 10

Amanda despised hospitals. She hated the squeaky linoleum floors, the ubiquitous blue chairs, the too-soothing voices the nurses always used. And she especially hated that antiseptic smell that permeated the halls—as if it could somehow sanitize the truth and erase the harsh reality of illness, insanity, death.

And now Claire was here, in this despicable place—and it was all her fault. While she'd been indulging the most exhilarating time of her life, lost in the pleasure of Luke's arms, her child was suffering from anaphylactic shock, being rushed to the emergency room where she could die.

No. Claire couldn't die. She refused to even think it. She stuffed down the fear, passed a nurse in her flowered scrubs and sneakers and hobbled even faster toward the emergency-room desk.

"My daughter's here," she breathlessly told the woman in charge. "Claire Patterson. She's in the emergency room."

"Through the double doors." The woman shifted her gaze to a spot behind her.

Amanda turned, relieved to see Luke heading toward her. They'd raced here from his penthouse, only pausing to throw on clothes—and he looked it. His T-shirt was wrinkled, his hair unruly. Morning whiskers coated his jaw. And despite the guarded look in his eyes, she was glad that he'd come in with her, that she didn't have to be here alone.

She didn't know why he'd suddenly withdrawn back at the penthouse. He'd shut down just before she'd received Kendall's phone call. But she couldn't deal with that now. Her emotions were bouncing all over the place, from guilt and dread, to remorse and fear. She'd think about the incredible night and Luke's odd reaction later on.

Desperate to see Claire, she limped through the double doors, past strangers waiting in wheelchairs, people groaning and crying on cots. By the time they found Claire in a curtained-off section, she was so worked up she wanted to wretch.

"Mommy," Claire wheezed, and Amanda's heart plummeted, the dread blasting back full force. Claire looked like a burn victim. Her face was puffed, her lips huge and distorted. Splotchy red welts covered her skin. She clung to Brownie, her eyes nearly swollen shut, looking so small and lost against the starched white sheets that it was all Amanda could do not to cry.

She rushed to Claire's side, set aside her crutches, and perched on the edge of the cot. "Oh, honey. What happened?" She pulled her into her arms, rested her cheek on her head, inhaled her little-girl scent.

Kendall rose from the plastic chair on the opposite side of the bed. "She had a reaction to the oatmeal."

"The oatmeal?" She frowned. How could that be?

"She was fine until then. I used the EpiPen, then brought her here."

Amanda rocked, dabbed the tears from Claire's blotchy face, then shot Kendall a questioning look. "You gave her the stuff from the plastic container, right?"

"Absolutely." Kendall's worried eyes stayed on Claire. "I gave her exactly what you told me. But it happened right after she ate the oatmeal, so that had to be it."

"I believe you." She pulled her gaze back to Claire. Kendall knew all about Claire's allergy to peanuts and understood how serious it was. She wouldn't have made a mistake.

But then how could this have happened? She screened every morsel Claire ate, refusing to even take a chance on commercial cereals. She was so scrupulous, in fact, that she hand mixed a special breakfast blend for Claire using oatmeal, walnuts and flax.

"The doctor will be back in a minute," Kendall added. "She gave her a shot of epinephrine. She said Claire's going to be fine."

"Thank you," she whispered. She cradled Claire closer, grateful that her sister had been there. But it should have been her. She never should have neglected her child—especially for a night of sex.

Guilt tightened her throat, and she glanced at Luke. He stood at the open curtain with his strong arms crossed, his rugged face set in grim lines.

She flashed back to the first time she'd seen him in the casino. Her impression of him had been exactly right—he was ruthless, powerful…predatory.

But he was far more complex than that. He had a tender side, a good side, no matter what he might think. He'd sheltered her. He'd saved her life on that hill. And she could never repay him for last night, for all that he'd taught her about herself. He'd given her an amazing gift, freeing her from the doubts and insecurities Wayne had instilled.

Still, he'd retreated after the shattering intimacy they'd shared. But maybe it was just as well. Claire's accident was a sobering reminder that nothing had really changed since she'd met him. They lived in different worlds.

Maybe he'd punched holes in her protective walls. Maybe he'd made her dream for a while about a man she could never have. But that's all it was, a dream. She had Claire to think about, possibly an illness to confront. No matter how much Luke compelled her, she couldn't turn a brief sexual interlude into a fairy-tale romance. And she certainly couldn't go off the deep end and let herself fall in love with the man.

But as she pulled her gaze from those carnal eyes, she feared that her heart had already taken the plunge.

Three hours later, Amanda settled her exhausted, drowsy daughter down for a nap. The doctor had pumped Claire full of antihistamines and adrenaline, making the welts fade, the dangerous swelling in her throat subside.

Amanda smoothed back Claire's wispy hair, rubbed her back, smiling at the sight of the bear peeking over the sheet. They'd been lucky today. They'd had a bad scare, nothing more. It could have been far worse.

And she had to make sure it didn't happen again. Determined to root out the source of the problem, she pushed aside her own exhaustion and rose.

She limped through the quiet house into the kitchen. Her sister had gone home. Luke had closeted himself in his office to make some calls. Only the tick of the grandfather clock in the hallway and the muted buzzing of gardeners trimming hedges by the pool broke the hush.

She propped her crutches against the counter and opened the pantry, then pulled out the cereal she'd mixed. She popped the top off the plastic container, sniffed and peered inside. No sign of peanuts that she could tell.

Frowning, she closed the container and put it back, then grabbed the can of walnuts from the shelf. She turned the can, looked at the label. *Peanuts.*

She stared at the can in disbelief. *Impossible.* She couldn't have used peanuts by mistake. She never bought them, never even allowed them in the house.

Stunned, she pried off the plastic lid, but there were peanuts inside. And the can was still nearly full, recently opened, just like the one she had used.

Still unwilling to believe it, she frantically searched the shelf. But there wasn't another can. These had to be the nuts she'd used.

Her mind reeling, she stumbled to the table and sank into a chair. How could she have done this? She couldn't have bought the wrong nuts and added them to Claire's food—could she? Because if she had… This was so much worse than misplacing a comb or forgetting where she'd parked the car. *She could have killed Claire.*

Horrified, she dropped her face into her hands. She dragged in a breath, tried to wrap her mind around what she had done. If she'd made this mistake, it proved she had her mother's illness, and it was progressing faster than she'd thought. She would need to tell Kendall, make preparations for Claire's future before she endangered her even more.

But she still couldn't believe it. How could she have done anything so careless? She searched for a different conclusion, desperate for something—anything—that would explain it away. But who else could have done it? Wayne was in Maryland. The police had even said so. And she refused to believe Kendall or Luke could have done anything this vicious to Claire.

Which put the blame back on her.

She pressed her hand to her lips and closed her eyes. She didn't want to face it, but neither could she keep ignoring the proof. She really was losing her mind.

She inhaled, trying to calm herself down, to ease the panic surging inside. Somehow she had to get through this and cope.

But then the muscles along the back of her neck tensed. The fine hairs on her forearms rose.

And she felt it again—that creeping, crawling sensation slithering over her skin. It wormed through her nerves, beat into her skull—that whisper of menace, danger. The feeling that he was back again, watching her.

She gasped air to her strangled lungs, tried to shove the paranoia away. Wayne wasn't here. She couldn't overreact. She had to get a grip on her nerves.

But the fright only mounted, mingled with dread. And she could feel him now, getting closer, closer....

She leaped up and whipped around. The kitchen was empty. Nothing moved. Only the grandfather clock ticked down the hallway, its beats sounding out the relentless chant: He's here. He's here. He's here.

"Who's there?" she croaked.

Silence echoed back.

"Who's there?" she cried again, and her voice rose to a shriek. Her knees began to shake. Terror poured through her cells. She pressed her hand to her throat, struggling not to come undone, but the fear mushroomed inside her, threatening to explode.

This had to be Wayne. He had to be here. She couldn't be losing her mind.

Could she?

She hugged her arms and rocked, let out an anguished moan.

She'd never felt more terrified or alone in her life.

Luke had never felt more out of control. He entered the kitchen a short time later, his gut in turmoil, a headache beating at the base of his skull. His entire life was unraveling before his eyes.

Sex with Amanda had shaken him, affected him in ways he didn't want to examine. The sight of her poor daughter swollen and blistered from that allergic reaction had bothered him even more.

He didn't want to care about them. He didn't want to get involved with Amanda or her child. He needed to focus on his project, on getting revenge on Harold Rothchild and attaining his goal.

Especially now that he'd gotten more bad news. Now even his project was slipping from his grasp—and to save it, he needed Amanda's help.

He spotted her slumped at the kitchen table, her hands covering her face. He hated telling her this latest development and adding to her stress when she was worried about Claire. But he didn't have much choice.

She was as caught up in this mess as he was. The police might even call her in for questioning now.

He slid into the chair across from her, and she lifted her head. His heart skidded at the torment in her eyes. "What happened? Is it Claire?"

She pushed her hair back from her face with trembling hands. "No. She's better. She's napping, but she's going to be fine."

"Then what's wrong?" Her face had paled. Fatigue puffed the skin around her eyes.

"Nothing." Her gaze flitted away. "I'm just tired."

"And I'm Santa Claus."

Her brows snapped together, and he scowled back. "Come on, Amanda. Don't give me that crap. You look like hell. You've been jumping at noises for days. Something's wrong, and I want to know what it is."

Her lips tightened. "It has nothing to do with you. It's just…something I have to deal with alone."

Her answer should have relieved him. He wanted to back away. He'd been trying to distance himself from this woman since the moment they'd met. But he'd be damned if he could do it. The thought of her suffering some private torment tore his insides to shreds.

He reached out and trapped her hand, caressing the fragile bones with his thumb. "Tell me, Amanda. Whatever it is, I'll help."

"You can't help," she whispered. "There's nothing anyone can do."

"Try me."

Her stricken eyes searched his. And he saw her hope, her doubt. The fear.

"Trust me," he said, and after an endless moment, she sighed.

"All right." She squeezed his hand, then tugged her own away. "But there's really nothing you can do. I told you I've been misplacing things."

"Yeah."

"Well, this time I put peanuts in Claire's oatmeal instead of walnuts. I could have killed her."

"So you made a mistake."

She rubbed her arms, looking even more distraught. "It's worse than that. I told you my mother was ill. But I didn't tell you…she was mentally ill, schizophrenic. She suffered from hallucinations, blackouts. She forgot things, did bizarre things—like putting the wrong ingredients in food."

Oh, hell. He sat back and folded his arms. No wonder she was upset. "You think you have the same thing."

She clasped her hands, gnawed at her bottom lip. "It can be genetic. And sometimes it doesn't show up until later in life, until your twenties and thirties."

"You're not mentally ill," he said flatly.

"But—"

"But nothing." He didn't believe it for a minute. "You told me this started after you moved here."

"Right. The night of Rothchilds' party. But—"

"Did anything happen last night at my penthouse?"

"No." A blush rose up her cheeks. "At least nothing like that."

Their gazes locked. Hunger rose and vibrated the air. His blood pulsed hard, and he battled back the urge to haul her across the table into his arms. This wasn't the time for sex.

He cleared his throat. "Look at it logically. All these events have happened in the house."

"Not the time I forgot where I parked."

"But you were here right before that. Someone could have followed you there."

"Maybe." Misery deadened her voice. "But I didn't black out here. That happened at the Rothchilds' casino."

She was right. He shoved his hand through his hair. "So there are inconsistencies. Let's not worry about that right now. Let's just assume someone is doing this to you."

"But—"

"Just assume for a minute."

"All right." She watched him, her forehead creased. And he wanted to hold her, comfort her, erase that anxiety from her face. He got to his feet, paced a safe distance away so he could think. "So who knows about your mother's illness?"

"Kendall, of course. And you do now."

"How about your ex?"

"Yes, but Wayne's in Maryland. He made his parole check. You told me that yourself."

Another detail they'd worry about later. "Tell me more about him."

"Like what?"

"How he acted. Things he did."

She leaned back in her chair, blew out her breath. "Well, he was a pretty classic abuser. When we were dating, he was charming. Extremely attentive. He sent flowers, gifts, made me feel special…desired."

She gave him an embarrassed smile. "I was actually flattered when he started acting possessive. I had no idea… And once I married him, it got worse. He alienated me from my friends, pressured me to quit my job. Then the criticisms started, the violent mood swings…"

"How did you get away?"

She shuddered. "It wasn't easy. He controlled everything, the car, the money. I started substitute teaching when he was out of town and put the money in a special escape fund."

He locked his jaw against the sudden rush of anger. Some day, he was going to confront that brute. He was going to make him pay for hurting her.

And if Wheeler was behind these problems now, that day would come soon.

"It got worse after I left," she said, and her voice wobbled. "The stalking, the phone calls. When I got those hang-up calls at Kendall's, I thought at first it was him. But it couldn't have been him. He wasn't the one in the casino. It wasn't his voice. And he had nothing to do with that ring."

Luke paced to the patio window, mulling that over. He stuffed his hands in his pockets, stared out at the sprinklers forming rainbows in the sun. This situation was complicated. There were too many threads, and none of them seemed to connect.

He turned back to Amanda. "I take it Wheeler knew you were worried about inheriting your mother's illness?" She nodded, confirming his suspicions. "Does Wheeler get custody of Claire if you're ill?"

"No, I don't think so. Not with his criminal record and the abuse. Kendall would take her." She grabbed her crutches and rose. "Even if he could, I can't see that as a motive. He never cared about her. The last thing he'd want holding him down is a child."

"But losing Claire would hurt you." A fact that Wheeler would know. Anyone could see how much she loved and protected her child. "And he knows about Claire's allergy?"

She stopped beside him, and her wide blue eyes searched his. "Yes. He knows everything about us, even that I mix that oatmeal."

"So what's your gut feeling? Is this something Wheeler would do?"

"This is exactly like him. When I had him arrested, he vowed to come after me, to make me pay. And I wish it were him. I'd much rather deal with Wayne than lose my mind. But it can't be him. He's in Maryland."

"So it would seem." He frowned out the window at the golf course beyond the patio. A couple of carts glided past.

"We know he didn't hold me up in the casino," she added. "And he wasn't on that hilltop, either. Unless there really is more than one person involved…" Her face paled, and she looked so spooked suddenly that he dreaded telling her the rest.

But she needed to know the truth. "I just got a phone call from my security chief, Matt Schaffer. He told me the notes definitely matched. The one you got was written by the same person who wrote to Harold Rothchild."

Her face went whiter yet. "So the killer was the one who took photos of Claire."

"It looks that way. It gets worse," he added as she pressed her fingers to her lips. "They've reopened the investigation. They originally arrested Matt's aunt, but she just turned out to be a nutcase."

She frowned, and he knew she still didn't understand. "This isn't public knowledge, but in the note Harold got, the killer vowed to get revenge on the family. That means I'm their prime suspect again."

"I don't see how. We told them about the man who

attacked us yesterday. You even described him. And we showed them the note I got and the surveillance tape."

"But I have a motive. And I've been involved in this from the start. You even got attacked in my casino."

"What a mess."

"Yeah." He exhaled. "It's a mess. But let's solve your problem first. I'll get Matt Schaffer on it. He can set up surveillance, find out if someone's entering the house and bypassing the security system."

Her eyes stayed on his. "And if no one is?"

"Then we'll deal with it." Unable to resist, he fitted his hands to her waist, stroked the gentle sweep of her spine. No matter what else was wrong in his life, no matter how much she distracted him from his goals, holding her still felt right. "Don't worry. We'll get through this."

"Thank you," she whispered. "I thought…I thought you'd be so disgusted if you knew. Wayne—"

"Do me a favor." He tilted her chin up. "Don't confuse me with that bastard again."

Her eyes turned dark, her lips soft. "I could never, ever confuse you with him."

He pulled her close, slanted his mouth over hers, making sure to drive that point home. He didn't know what the future held. His life and emotions were in upheaval. But like it or not, last night had changed things. And for this moment at least, she was his.

He ended the kiss before it got out of hand, and pressed her head to his neck. And for a long moment he just stood there with her in his arms. Her warm, supple body curved against his. Her soft breath caressed his skin. He breathed in her womanly scent, feeling the inevitable lust build in his veins.

But then a thought intruded—the reason he'd sought her out. He had a party to attend that night. He needed to put on a good face, subdue the rumors Matt's crazy aunt's release would cause. And he needed Amanda by his side.

But Claire was sick, and he knew Amanda wouldn't leave her yet. He didn't have to ask. He'd seen the dismay in her eyes at the hospital, knew that she blamed herself.

And he couldn't leave them here alone. Candace's killer was on the loose. Wheeler could be lurking around, bypassing his security system and getting into the house. That thought made his blood run cold.

He could move her into his penthouse, but then Wheeler wouldn't show up. And they needed proof he was toying with her so they could trap him and end this mess.

He exhaled, knowing he didn't have a choice. He had to risk fueling the rumors and miss the event. He had to stay here and protect Amanda and Claire.

It could jeopardize his project, he knew that. The investors might see his absence as guilt.

But as his mouth devoured hers again, and he surrendered to the passion clouding his mind, his only concern was pleasuring her.

Chapter 11

Luke believed her. He didn't think she was losing her mind.

Amanda sank into the steamy kiss, her mind reeling, her heart flooded with gratitude to this man. He hadn't recoiled at the mention of her mother's illness, hadn't turned from her in disgust. If ever she'd needed proof that Luke was a thousand times better than Wayne, he'd just provided it in spades.

And she knew at that moment, that she was hopelessly, irrevocably in love with him.

His mouth covered hers, his tongue making deep, bold sweeps of her mouth, and she tightened her grip on his neck. She loved everything about him—his strength and self-assurance, his gruff tenderness. And the thrilling, arousing feel of him drove her wild.

She kissed him back, her heart overloaded with emotions, showing him how much his confidence meant. She ached for him, hungered for him, wanting to get closer yet. Feeling brazen, she rubbed her hips against his, and the long, rigid length of him made her moan. He laughed softly against her mouth.

He gentled the kiss, slid his lips to her jaw, her neck, sending pleasure streaming over her skin. "I'm addicted to you," he rasped.

"I can't stop, either," she confessed. She slid her hands over his hard, muscled shoulders to the short, silky hairs on the back of his neck. His whiskered jaw brushed her cheek, and excitement rushed through her veins.

He bent down slightly, wrapped his arms around her waist, then lifted her into his arms. She gasped at his strength, clutched his shoulders for balance as he turned with her and strode down the hall.

He carried her into her bedroom, kicked the door closed, then lowered her onto the bed. "Claire—" she began.

"I'll check on her. Don't move." He crossed the room and opened the adjoining door. He peeked into Claire's bedroom, then eased the door shut again. "She's asleep." He threw the bolt to lock them in.

Then he returned to the bed, looking predatory suddenly. He planted his feet wide, braced his hands low on his hips. The hungry look in his eyes made her tremble with need.

He stood there, watching her for a long, tense moment, as if debating how to proceed. "Since you can't stop," he said slowly. "Why don't you show me what you need?"

Her breath caught. Awareness rippled through her, and she realized what he wanted her to do. She nibbled her lip, suddenly uncertain, not sure if she had the courage. A week ago, she never would have dared.

But a week ago she'd been insecure about her sexuality, cowed by Wayne's cruel criticism, trapped in a cage of self-doubt.

Luke had unlocked that cage, set her free. And she refused to let her fears imprison her again.

She eyed the heat smoldering in his eyes, the hard set to his jaw, the definite bulge in his slacks. A delicious sense of abandon overtook her. The old Amanda was gone. Now she was going to shock him—shock herself—and take a risk. For once, she wasn't going to define herself by her doubts.

She scooted back on the bed, careful not to bump her injured ankle, then defiantly lifted her chin. And then she slowly dragged off her T-shirt and tossed it aside. She made much shorter work of her bra.

Luke didn't move. His gaze dropped to her breasts, the burn in them scalding her skin. Encouraged, she closed her eyes, let her head fall back, and cupped her breasts with her hands. And then she imagined Luke's hands instead of her own, how he'd touch and fondle and stroke, the feel of his rough, masculine palms, the scorching heat of his mouth. Her breathing grew fast, shivers sparked over her skin as her hands mimicked what she saw in her mind.

She arched back, opened her eyes. He stood frozen at the foot of the bed, his gaze riveted on her breasts. His body had gone rigid. A muscle flexed his jaw. His eyes were hot, dangerous, dark.

Good.

She sank back against the pillows. Keeping her eyes glued on his face, she inched off her shorts. Her underpants dropped to the floor next. His eyes tracked every move.

She paused, naked now, and battled a sudden flurry of nerves. She felt embarrassed, uncertain. But this was Luke, the man who believed in her.

"You're not stopping now." The rough tone of his voice made her shiver with need.

"No," she whispered back. "I'm not stopping now. I want you too much."

"Show me," he said.

She parted her thighs, showed him exactly what she wanted, responding to the slow sliding strokes of her hand. A heavy fullness rippled through her. The need grew into an ache, stripping away the last of her inhibitions.

He stood rooted in place, his hands clenched into fists, following every motion she made. Her skin grew tight. Her entire body tensed. She shuddered, lost in his eyes, willing him closer, needing his hands…his mouth.

"Luke," she whispered, the need unbearable now. And she couldn't stop. The hunger built and swelled, the need for him beyond her control. She breathed faster, harder, wanting him with a wildness she couldn't contain.

"Luke," she cried out again, and then she bucked hard, exploding with pleasure while he still stood immobile and watched.

Suddenly, he erupted into a flurry of action. He ripped off his shirt, kicked off his pants, tossing them to the floor. And then he knelt above her, plunging into her in one hard stroke, bringing her back to the brink. She gasped at the delicious invasion, thrilled to his hard, pulsating feel. He buried himself to the hilt, filling her, claiming her.

"That was the sexiest thing I've ever seen," he said, his voice hoarse.

He kissed her, plundering deeply with his tongue,

searing her with his blatant need. His muscles rippled under her palms. His wide shoulders bunched and strained. The kiss was fierce, provoking, and she kissed him back with everything she had.

Then her body grew taut, the ache unbearable. She moaned against his mouth. He thrust hard, and she combusted in an explosion of bliss. His deeper groans mingled with hers.

For several, long moments, neither moved. Breathing erratically, she trailed her fingertips over the stubble shadowing his jaw and traced the hollows of his cheeks.

He braced himself on his forearms, and she inhaled deeply, relishing his masculine scent. His gaze roamed her lips, her breasts. And then his eyes trapped hers, kicking off a riot of emotions in her chest.

"Do you have any idea how erotic that was?" he asked.

She trembled, shocked that she already wanted him again. She didn't think she could get enough. But it wasn't just the sex, she realized suddenly. His masculine virility compelled her, but it was his essence that captivated her heart.

Her throat closed on a sudden pang of longing, her love for him brimming in her chest. Not wanting him to see how vulnerable she felt, she averted her gaze, stroked the wide line of his shoulders, the firm muscles bulging beneath his sleek skin.

"You've done so much for me," she managed to say around the thickness in her throat. "I can never begin to repay you."

He tipped up her chin, but she kept her gaze lowered, afraid to expose the feelings she knew would show in her eyes. She traced the edge of his beard stubble, loving how sexy he looked with those straight, dark brows, those masculine lips.

"I know some ways you could try."

The seductive tone of his voice caught her attention, and she braved a glance at his face. His golden eyes gleamed with humor, and her heart warmed even more. "Is that a promise?" she asked.

"Count on it."

She loved this playful side of him, a side he rarely revealed. But she understood why he kept it hidden. She'd grown up just as he had, shouldering the weight of responsibility, facing the harsh realities of life at a too-young age.

She'd felt the same hopelessness, bitterness, the consuming need to survive. But she'd accepted her life, let go of the pain. She couldn't fight her mother's mental illness. There wasn't a concrete enemy to blame.

But Luke had a target—Harold Rothchild. That fury had sustained him, along with his all-consuming ambition and drive. And she understood his need for vengeance, for respect. She even understood why he feared letting people close.

She frowned, trailed her hand over the tendons running down his shoulder and arm. But waging a constant war took its toll. It hurt his enemies, and it hurt him. Even innocent people got trapped in the fight.

Like the people living in the slums he was going to destroy.

She nibbled her lip, knowing she would do anything this man asked. She just had. And she'd help him get that project approved if that's what he needed most. But maybe she could convince him not to go through with it, to let go of his need for revenge.

To let the pain heal.

He pulsed inside her, and her breath caught. His mouth went to her breast and ignited her hunger again. She closed her eyes, plunged her hands in his thick, silky hair, felt him move his body down hers. And then she didn't think at all.

Luke sprawled on the sofa the next morning, every inch of his body relaxed. He'd never felt so content in his life. Sex with Amanda just kept getting better. She continually surprised him, making him want to hole up with her somewhere and not emerge for months.

He passed a hand over his gritty eyes, pulled out his BlackBerry and yawned. She'd kept him so enthralled he hadn't thought about work for hours—the first time that had happened in years. He checked the phone log, saw that he'd missed a call from his security chief. He punched in Matt's number and waited for him to pick up.

He glanced at Claire playing on the carpet near his feet. The kid had made a full recovery and was busy chattering at her bear. It was just as well that she demanded attention. Without Claire to distract Amanda, he'd never get anything done.

"Schaffer here," Matt said.

Luke got right to the point. "Did you get anything?"

"Yeah. We struck pay dirt. One of the gardeners entered your house early this morning."

Luke went still. His eyes swerved to the window overlooking the pool. The thought of someone skulking around the hallways while he and Amanda slept made everything inside him cold. It was a good thing she'd been with him all night.

He lowered his voice so Amanda and Claire wouldn't hear. "Where is he now?"

"I don't know. He didn't stay inside long."

"How's he getting in?"

"He used the patio entrance this time. He bypassed the system, but he obviously didn't know about the new cameras we installed."

Luke went from the couch to the patio, examined the door. "There's no sign of forced entry."

"He's using the codes. We're checking on how he got them now. And he fits the description you provided—stocky, blond hair."

Wheeler. Satisfaction curled through him, merging with the deep, scorching rage. It was past time to confront that creep.

"Don't notify the police," he told Matt. He needed to think this through, set a trap. "And don't change the codes—we don't want to tip him off."

"All right."

"I'll talk to Amanda and clear it with her, but I want to catch him today." He scowled at a sudden thought. He had another meeting with the investors that afternoon. But he'd just have to postpone it again.

"Got it," Matt said. "By the way, Natalie decided to put me out of my misery and agreed to a wedding date. Mark your calendar for June fourteenth, here in Vegas."

Luke grinned. "I'll be there."

He disconnected the line and slipped his Black-Berry into the pocket of his slacks. So Matt and Natalie were going to tie the knot soon. He'd suspected as much. Their whirlwind romance had made the tabloids, lending credence to the rumors about that missing diamond ring's weird curse—that in the right hands, it brought true love. In the wrong hands, chaos ensued.

His gaze bee-lined to Amanda where she sat at the kitchen table. Her soft, shiny hair tumbled over her arms. Her snug T-shirt cupped her breasts. His gaze lingered, memories of how her skin had tasted stirring his blood. Just watching her filled him with a sense of rightness.

He'd never thought about getting married, never wanted to. But he suddenly understood Matt. The idea of having Amanda around for a while appealed to him—sleeping in her arms every night, waking up with her every day.

He frowned and angled his head, rolling that idea over in his mind. Maybe she wouldn't be in a hurry to leave when this was done. Maybe he could convince her to stay, at least for a while. This woman had a lot of facets he still wanted to explore.

His body stirring, he kept his gaze on her breasts. He had plans for her, all right.

But first they had to catch her ex-husband.

Amanda dragged her attention away from Luke at the patio door to the teaching application in her hands. She stared at the paper blindly, her brain still fried, unable to stop thinking about the rapturous night. She had to pull herself together, though. She was acting like a lovestruck teenager, mooning over him, reliving those delirious sensations he'd evoked.

She exhaled, blowing her loose hair back from her face. She loved Luke, but she had to be practical. He'd never mentioned any feelings for her, especially not love. All she knew for sure right now was that he wanted her sexually.

My, had he driven *that* point home. She closed her eyes, shivering at the erotic memories—his muscles flexing under her palms, his eyes blazing with need. The thrill of having all that power and intensity focused only on her. And the things he'd asked her to do. Her face warmed. She'd never known she had such a wanton streak.

But desiring her sexually didn't mean he loved her. He'd never proposed marriage, never mentioned a future together. Which meant she had to get herself back on track.

She looked at the front room, where Luke squatted down, talking to Claire. And Amanda knew she had to tread carefully. She'd made a big mistake with Wayne. Thanks to her faulty judgment, her daughter's life was at stake.

Luke wasn't Wayne. He wasn't even close. She would never believe the rumors about his supposed role in Candace's murder.

But he was definitely out of her league. And it wasn't just her own feelings she had to protect. Claire could end up attached to him, hurt when they had to leave.

Which meant she couldn't draw this out. She had to make plans, quickly find a job.

Luke rose in a fluid motion, then came toward her. Her gaze stalled on his powerful thighs, the way his shirt clung to his muscled abs. Her throat went dry at the sight.

She frowned at the application again. She had it bad, all right. She understood why that murdered woman had stalked him—especially now that she'd spent two nights in his bed. He was addictive, the perfect man. How could she settle for anyone else again?

"What are you doing?" he asked, sliding into the seat next to hers.

"Filling out a job application. There's an opening for a middle school history teacher."

"That doesn't sound exciting."

She shrugged, trying to keep her mind on the conversation instead of him. "It's a good job, and the school's not far from Kendall's house."

He leaned closer, and his nearness made it hard to breathe. "I thought you wanted to be an archaeologist."

She straightened the papers into a stack. "So?"

"So why don't you go for it?"

She shifted her gaze to Claire, watched her balance Brownie on the back of the couch. "It's not practical. I'd have to go back to school, do research. It would take years. And I have Claire to think about."

Besides, some dreams just weren't meant to be...like staying with him.

He looked as if he intended to argue, but then he shrugged. "I just spoke to Matt Schaffer."

Her pulse sped up. "What did he say?"

"The surveillance tape shows a gardener entering the house earlier today. He matches Wheeler's description."

She closed her eyes, clamped her hand over her lips. And the dread squeezing her chest began to ease.

"So it wasn't me," she whispered. "I really wasn't imagining things."

"No." He caught her hand in his, and gently squeezed. "You're as sane as I am, for what it's worth."

Tears misted her eyes, and her voice broke. "Luke... This is... I can't begin to thank you."

She inhaled, trying to hold back the emotions ricocheting inside. She didn't have her mother's illness. She wouldn't lose Claire. She was free.

And Luke had done this for her. He'd believed in her, helped her get proof.

She sniffed, grappling to stay in control, and wiped a tear from her eye. "How did he get by his parole officer?"

"I don't know. We'll find that out later. But you need to make a decision."

"What do you mean?"

"You have a couple of choices. We can contact the police right now and have him arrested."

He'd go to jail. But eventually he'd get released. And she'd be watching over her shoulder again, always waiting. The terror would never end. "What's the other choice?"

"We set a trap and confront him first, and then call the police."

Confront him. She'd have to see Wayne face-to-face? She tried not to panic at the thought. "What good would that do?"

He leaned back in his chair and folded his arms. "I'm going to put this baldly. He thinks he owns you. In his mind, you're his." His gaze held hers. "He's never going to stop trying to control you—especially since you defied him by getting away."

She shivered, his words chilling her. But Luke was right. Wayne had vowed to make her pay. "But then—"

"That's where I come in. I'll make it clear to him that you're mine now. That's how he thinks, Amanda. It's the only way he's going to let you go. You don't have to do anything," he added. "Just be the bait. You get him here, and then I'll make sure he understands."

She saw the anger simmering in Luke's eyes, the rage. He could do it. He could finally put an end to this perpetual fear.

But only if she had the courage to reel Wayne in.

She glanced at Claire. Her daughter stood clutching her bear now, watching her with anxious eyes.

Her anger flared. Claire didn't deserve this, and neither did she—the constant fear, the years of abuse. He'd even followed her here.

And he'd gone way too far when he'd poisoned Claire. That had been the final straw. It was time to bring this reign of terror to an end.

She locked eyes with Luke. "Let's set the trap."

Chapter 12

The waiting was killing her.

Amanda lay on one of the lounge chairs by the pool, feeling defenseless and exposed in her modest swimsuit, her stomach threatening to revolt. On the surface, the afternoon seemed perfectly peaceful. Insects droned from the nearby hedge. The soft breeze brushed her skin. Beyond the golf course, heat shimmered up from the desert floor, forming a wavering, watery mirage. But Wayne could show up any time now, and it was tearing her insides to shreds.

She focused her gaze on the distant mountains, forced herself to calm down. Nothing would go wrong. They'd gone over this a dozen times. She was not to provoke Wayne into an argument, was not to go anywhere with him—not even into the house. She'd just speed dial the cell phone the second she saw him and let Luke take it from there.

She patted the corner of the towel where she'd tucked the cell phone, squinted at the sparkling pool. Kendall had spirited Claire to the safety of Luke's penthouse. Luke waited just outside the compound, expecting her call. She glanced at her watch, her anxiety mounting as the minutes wore on. What if Wayne didn't show up?

He'd better come. She needed to end this today. She refused to spend day after endless day waiting, not knowing what he would do.

Her skin clammy despite the heat. She sipped her glass of lemonade, trying to soothe her parched throat. Then she flipped the page on the magazine she had in her lap in an attempt to look relaxed.

And then she smelled it—Wayne's scent. It wisped through the air and crept into her nostrils like smoke from a smoldering fire. She kept her eyes glued to the magazine, her heart accelerating into overdrive, her senses hyperalert.

Was that him? Was he behind her? Or had she imagined that scent? She inhaled but only smelled the chlorine from the pool. She didn't dare turn around to check.

Instead she reached for the lemonade again, brought the glass to her lips with a trembling hand. *Stop shaking,* she ordered herself fiercely. *Don't let him see your fear.*

The smell grew stronger. He was definitely behind her. Her breath wheezed out.

She had to call Luke fast.

She set the glass carefully on the table, reached for the phone under the towel. But a gun barrel was pressed against her temple, and she went dead still.

"That's right," Wayne said from behind her, and the sound of his voice made her nausea rise. "Now stand up, nice and slow, or you'll be dead."

She heard the rage in his voice the awful excitement. He actually wanted to kill her. He thought he had the right.

And she only had a second to act. She flicked her gaze to the towel, trying not to move her head. Then she stretched her fingers toward the cell phone, reaching... reaching.

The gun bit into her skin. "Pick up that phone and I shoot. Now get up."

Panic mingling with disbelief, she rose on quivering legs. This couldn't be happening. She couldn't let it. She had to follow the plan...

The gun eased away, and her hopes spiked. But Wayne circled into view, his weapon still aimed at her head. The stench of aftershave assaulted her senses, and she went rigid with fear.

Think, she urged herself fiercely. *Think.* She couldn't let him do this to her.

His face leered close and she forced herself to look. His skin was flushed. A bead of sweat crawled down his jaw. Hatred gleamed in his mean blue eyes.

How had she ever thought him handsome? How had she ever believed she could care for this man?

"I told you I'd make you pay," he said, and the violence in his voice congealed her blood. He moved closer, and his hot breath sickened her gut.

Without warning, he slammed the gun against her head. She cried out, slumped to her knees.

Stunned, blinded by pain, she gasped for air. Oh, God. This was worse than she'd expected. He was vicious, out of control. And she knew with a bone deep certainty that he wasn't going to let her live.

She staggered back to her feet. She battled the spasms in her injured ankle, the violent ache in her head. Blood trickled into her eye. Wayne circled her again, preparing to strike.

And suddenly, anger sparked inside her, outrage that this creep thought he could terrorize her. So what if she got hurt when she defied him? She refused to feed his ego again.

She stepped back, pretending to cower, moving close to the lemonade glass. "Don't," she whimpered, knowing it was what he expected from her.

He flashed that sadistic grin. She took another step back, pressed her too-slick palms to her thighs. "Please don't hurt me," she whispered again. He stepped toward her, and she knew that she'd run out of time.

She switched her gaze to a spot behind him. He fell for the trick and glanced back. She grabbed the glass of lemonade, flung the stinging liquid into his eyes.

He blinked, growled with anger. She hurled the heavy tumbler at his head. The glass bounced off his skull, but it momentarily stunned him, then shattered on the tiles at his feet. Her pulse frantic, she lunged for the phone on the chair.

It didn't matter. Luke vaulted the hedge, slammed into Wayne. The two men crashed to the ground.

Wayne didn't have a chance. Luke rammed Wayne's head against the tiles, punched his face and gut in a flurry of fists. Wayne groaned, cried out. The sickening thuds made her cringe.

But Luke was relentless, fighting with a fury she'd never seen. Within seconds, Wayne lay motionless and was bleeding on the ground, the gun a safe distance away.

Luke rammed his knee into Wayne's throat. "Leave her alone," he ordered. He shoved down harder, and

Wayne let out a helpless wheeze. "She's mine now. Amanda and Claire are mine. Do you hear me?" Wayne's face turned purple, and he gasped for air. "You come near them again and you're dead."

Wayne croaked out his agreement. Luke pressed down for a few more seconds, then finally released him and stood.

Her heart still thundering, Amanda dragged in a shaky breath. Then she walked to where her ex-husband lay. And for a long moment she just stared at him, this man who'd caused her such terror, such pain. He'd seemed so powerful once, so cunning and brutally strong. Now he was just bloody, pathetic, cowed.

And she realized it was over. It was finally over. She was free of Wayne at last.

Luke stood in his casino's ballroom that evening, his words still echoing in his head. *She's mine,* he'd told Wheeler. *Amanda and Claire are mine.* He'd meant the words only for show, to keep Wheeler from bothering them again. But the hell of it was, those words sounded right. Amanda did feel like his.

He glanced at her across the crowded ballroom, watched her fill her small plate with hors d'oeuvres. She wore a thigh-high black dress that molded her curves, showcasing those killer legs. The front was modest, but tight, the fabric cupping her breasts like a lover's hands. But in the back… The dress plunged dramatically to her hips, riveting every man's gaze to her tempting, naked skin.

His throat suddenly dry, he took a swallow of whiskey. He'd touched that skin, made love to every inch of that sensual body. He knew her scent, her taste.

He knew what made her moan, what made her sigh, how her flesh felt hot and moist. He'd made her swollen and aching with need.

She was beautiful, erotic.

And she was his.

She could have died today. Every time he closed his eyes, he flashed back to the image of her bloody scalp, the deranged look in Wheeler's eyes, and the frantic need to protect her consumed him all over again.

"Is the meeting still on for tomorrow?" a man standing beside him asked.

Luke tossed back his last swallow of whiskey, pulled his attention to Fletcher Coddington. The elderly investor's wife was with him tonight, and the voluptuous young woman smiled up at Luke, the invitation clear in her eyes. Luke scanned her collagen-plumped lips, her silicone breasts, the fake, come-hither smile. Maybe the giant rock on her finger was phony, too. It would serve her right.

He looked back at Amanda. She turned his way, smiling at something someone said, and his heart made a swerve in his chest. She was the exact opposite of Coddington's gold-digging wife—authentic, interesting, sincere.

"Montgomery?" Coddington said, sounding annoyed.

He jerked his eyes back to the investor, scrambling to remember what he'd said. The meeting. Right. "It's all set. Ten o'clock tomorrow." It was their final meeting, the day they'd sign the contracts on the Phoenix project and decide if it was a go. The day he'd toll the death knell for Harold Rothchild.

At last.

And he had Amanda to thank for it. Once again, she'd

soothed the investors with her warm smile and gentle voice. She'd diffused questions about the murder, showed everyone her confidence in him. And he knew damn well she'd kept several worried men from backing out.

She looked up then, and her eyes met his from across the room. That familiar heat jolted through him, that feeling of rightness.

"Excuse me," he said and headed toward her, leaving Coddington sputtering behind.

He worked his way through the chattering crowd, ignoring bids for his attention, anxious to get to her side. And that deep sense of possessiveness settled inside him again. He didn't know when it had started, only that it was there—and was growing stronger each day.

The scare today had clinched it. He realized he didn't want Amanda to leave, didn't want her moving back to her sister's house, even when the danger was gone. She belonged with him now.

And it was time to make that clear.

Amanda's pulse quickened as Luke strode toward her across the glittering ballroom, those bourbon-colored eyes locked on hers. Lord, he looked sexy. His broad shoulders filled out his tuxedo. Light from the enormous chandeliers glinted off his ebony hair. His stark-white shirt set off his tanned skin, and he looked so unapologetically masculine, so utterly sensual that thrills of excitement skipped through her nerves.

Breathless, she dropped her gaze to her plate. She had to get a grip. It was bad enough that she was in love with him. She couldn't embarrass them both by ogling him in a public place.

Not that every other woman in the room wasn't doing the same.

A waiter materialized at her side. "Wine?" he asked.

Startled, she studied the waiter's face. But he was too short, too dark to be the man who'd drugged her the other night.

"No, thanks," she said, and he moved on. She doubted anyone would try to attack her tonight, but she wasn't drinking, just to be safe—especially with Candace's killer still on the loose.

At least Wayne was no longer a problem. She nibbled on a crab-stuffed mushroom, relieved that he was locked up. He'd been arrested and charged with a litany of crimes—breaking and entering, stalking, committing numerous parole violations, including possessing a firearm and crossing state lines. He'd stay in prison for years. And when he did get out, he would leave her alone...thanks to Luke.

Luke joined her just then. Adrenaline raced through her veins. She wondered if she'd ever feel normal around him. Every time she looked at him, her pulse went amok.

"Join me on the balcony?" he asked.

"Sure." Her appetite gone, she set down the plate and took his arm. They strolled from the noisy ballroom, moving slowly because of her still-tender ankle.

And suddenly, a thought came out of nowhere, catching her off guard. Maybe he was going to end their arrangement now. Wayne had been arrested. Tomorrow his project would be approved and he no longer needed her help. Candace's killer was still at large, but surely the police would catch him soon.

Which meant Luke might want their masquerade to end.

Her breath fled in a surge of panic. It was too soon for her. Way too soon and not only because of the danger. She needed time to show Luke how much she loved him. Time to heal him from his past pain. Time to convince him to change his mind about the project, to let go of the bitterness and his need for revenge.

"Down here." He led her across the spacious balcony, away from prying ears. And with every step, her anxiety mounted. If he wanted to end it now, what could she say?

They reached the far corner of the balcony, and he stopped. She braced her hands on the railing to collect herself, looking out at the dazzling array of lights. Neon signs glittered and flashed. Honking horns and the muted roar of traffic drifted up.

And a terrible emptiness lodged inside her, threatening to destroy what little composure she had left. But she had only herself to blame for this mess. She'd known better than to fall in love with Luke. He'd been a fantasy from the start, completely unattainable. She'd known that it would end.

Which was poor comfort to her breaking heart.

"I've been thinking," he began, and she closed her eyes, determined to accept her fate with dignity.

"Now that Wheeler's out of the picture, you could stay with me. Move in for real."

Shock rippled through her. She opened her eyes and searched his face, not sure that she'd heard him right. She'd expected him to end their affair, not invite her to stay. "You want me to live with you?"

"There's no reason you have to go back to your sister's house, is there?"

Her lips parted. Confusion still muddled her mind.

"No, but…" This didn't sound very romantic. It was hardly the declaration of love she yearned for. "I…I don't know."

"What don't you know? It makes sense for you to stay. You need a place to live. And we're good together, Amanda." He crowded against her, tugged up her chin. The heat from his body seeped through her skin. "Very good."

He smoothed her hair away from her neck, lowered his mouth to the sensitive skin. She shivered at the sensual touch and closed her eyes, the familiar desire whipping through her like a blast of sand in a desert storm. They were more than good together. They burned.

Her head fell back. Her knees turned weak. He leaned into her, and she shuddered at the hard bulge pressing the juncture of her thighs.

She longed to obey her body's mandate. She ached to take him inside her and tell him yes. She wanted to feel that shocking pleasure every night, the exhilaration of his kiss every day. And she loved him madly. Staying with him was the answer to her dreams.

Almost. He hadn't mentioned marriage or love.

Trying to think through the hunger muddling her brain, she wrenched herself away. She pressed her fingers to her forehead, gazed out at the colorful display of lights.

His offer was tempting. Too tempting. She loved him and owed him so much. He'd awakened her sexually, freed her from Wayne. He'd even risked his life to save hers.

But he didn't love her.

Maybe with time she could make him love her, though. Maybe she could heal him and pay him back.

Maybe if she lived with him, she could convince him to let go of the bitterness, move on from the painful past.

Or maybe she was deluding herself again.

She drew in a breath of air, tried to think this through. She'd made a terrible mistake with Wayne. When she'd found herself pregnant, she'd taken a risk. Even though she hadn't known him well, she'd decided that love and compassion would come with time.

She'd been wrong. Horribly wrong.

She couldn't afford to make another mistake. She didn't only have her own heart at risk this time but Claire's. Her daughter already adored Luke. And before she would let Claire become even more attached, she needed a sign he was willing to change. She couldn't act only on faith, no matter how tempted she was.

"Luke…" She turned to face him again. He watched her with narrowed eyes. "Do you think your project will be approved?"

He planted his hands on his hips and frowned, the abrupt change of subject obviously taking him aback. "We're signing the contracts tomorrow. The investors are all on board."

She hugged her arms, looked out at the area just past the Strip where Naked City was. Not many lights twinkled there.

"Thanks for your help, by the way."

She nodded, then glanced at him again. "The thing is…I'm not sure I did the right thing by helping you. With your project, I mean."

His brow furrowed. "What are you talking about?"

"It's just… It bothers me that those people are going to lose their homes."

"They'll find another place to live."

"But where? What place? Prices are sky high here in Vegas. You know that. They'll end up on the streets."

He crossed his arms, falling into stony silence, and she tried again. "We got kicked out of our apartment when I was growing up. You said you did, too. Don't you remember what it was like? That awful fear?"

"I remember." His eyes turned cold. "Harold Rothchild was our landlord. He took away my mother's job, her house. He killed her with his indifference. And now he's going to pay."

Her heart chilled at the vengeance in his voice. He didn't understand. "But you're doing the same thing he did. There are children in those slums, Luke. Innocent children."

"Forget it," he warned her.

"But—"

"Stay out of this, Amanda." His tone turned hard. "I'm not shelving this project. Not for you, not anyone."

"But that's just it," she whispered. "This revenge… It's not good for you. Not healthy. It's eating you up inside. You have to let go of it, move on from the past."

"Right." He made a sound of disgust. "You mean like you have?"

She flinched at the sarcasm in his voice. "Yes, I—"

"You what? You think you've moved on?" His eyes turned so angry that her throat closed up. "Hell, you're so stuck in the past you're afraid to live your life. Why don't you forget that damn teaching job? Go back to school and become what you want. Start living for yourself for a change."

"But it's not the same thing. I can't just do what I

want. I have responsibilities—Claire. She needs stability, security. I don't have a choice."

He slowly shook his head. "There's always a choice. And you're choosing to stay in the past. You're too scared to take a chance."

The accusation stung. A dull ache pounded her skull. This wasn't about her. It was about him. How had this conversation gone so wrong? "Won't you at least think about it? Delay the project a bit?"

"No. It's all set. I'm not changing my mind."

Her heart plummeted. "Then I…I can't live with you, Luke."

"Because of the project." His voice sounded dead.

"No, it's not just that." Oh, God. She'd made a total hash of this thing. And she couldn't let it end like this. She had to take a risk, make sure he understood.

She dredged up her courage, laid her soul bare. "I don't want to just live together, Luke. I want it all—marriage, a ring, love. I want to have your children someday. And I want you to forget revenge."

His eyes turned even colder. "I'm not proposing marriage."

And she couldn't delude herself into thinking he would change. "Then there's nothing more to say."

He stared at her for a long moment. She thought she was going to be sick. What on earth had just happened? How could he not understand?

"You can stay in the house until the end of the week," he said. "I'll hire you a bodyguard and get a security system installed in Kendall's house to keep you safe."

He turned from her, strode back toward the balcony door. And then he stopped and glanced back. His glacial expression shattered her heart. "I'll call you a cab."

She swayed, clung to the balcony railing, desolation clutching her throat.

And watched the man she loved walk away.

Chapter 13

At one o'clock on a Saturday morning, Las Vegas Boulevard throbbed with life. Flashing lights lured gamblers into casinos. Thrill rides shot riders a hundred stories above the ground. Inebriated tourists milled in and out of strip clubs, spending their hard-earned dollars on shows.

Naked City teemed, too, but the action here was edgier, seedier, far more deadly.

Luke pulled his Jaguar up to the curb in front of his old apartment and cut the engine, then pushed open the door and climbed out. He paused, inhaled the stench of rotting garbage, stepped over the broken glass and trash. Chain link fences locked off the aging, one-story buildings. Graffiti covered the peeling stucco walls. In front of a motel sign missing half its letters stood an overflowing Dumpster, gang tags spray painted on its side.

Not sure what the hell he was doing here, Luke

scowled at the rundown apartments, the ripped-up sofa someone had dumped on the curb. He'd tried to bury himself in work after he'd left the party, tried to fine tune the contracts for the meeting later that day, but Amanda's rejection ate at him, destroying his focus. He'd finally given up and gone for a drive.

He'd ended up here.

And it ticked him off. He didn't want to look at his old neighborhood, didn't want to keep remembering what Amanda had said. She'd been out of line. The Phoenix project had nothing to do with the two of them. She had no idea what this meant to him, how many years he'd worked for this revenge.

He leaned back against the Jaguar and folded his arms, studied the trio of teens strolling toward him from down the street. The faces had changed over time, but Naked City still reeked of the same poverty and violence, the same desperate need to survive.

The teens stopped several yards away and eyed him. Their leader, a kid in pants with its crotch hanging down to his knees, swaggered over. He looked young, maybe all of thirteen with his baseball cap on backward and that peach fuzz gracing his lip.

But the kid sized him up with a worldly expression Luke knew well. He'd been just like that kid once—scared, hungry, too street savvy at an early age. And that's when he'd decided to leave this place. He'd stood right here, gazing at the high-rise casinos glittering on the nearby Strip, vowing to be someone, to never be hungry or powerless again.

And he'd worked his butt off to do it. He'd studied hard, landed a scholarship to a private high school, walked miles every morning to get himself there. He'd made connections at that school, learned how to work the system, taught himself to fit in with a better crowd. And then he'd started making money—lots of it—until he was wealthier than he'd ever dreamed.

But he'd never lost sight of his plan to take down Harold Rothchild.

And in a few more hours, he would succeed.

The kid stuffed his hands in his back pockets, glanced around. "You looking to score?"

Luke eyed the kid's scrawny frame, his hollowed-out cheeks, the desperation in his eyes. "No."

The kid moved closer, his gaze flitting to the Jaguar and back. "I can get good stuff."

"I'm not here for drugs."

The kid nodded. "You want some action. Gina's real hot. I'll go find her for twenty bucks."

The edge of Luke's mouth kicked up. The kid hadn't missed a beat. But then, kids learned early how to wheel and deal on the streets. They bartered for everything—drugs, sex, food, even their lives.

And suddenly, it struck him that he hadn't changed much. He was still cutting deals like this kid was, only with more money and higher stakes.

That thought knocked him off balance. Maybe he hadn't left this life behind. Maybe he was the same punk he'd been back then, just with a more sophisticated veneer.

A low-riding car rumbled up the street then, its shiny chrome flashing, its booming stereo vibrating the soles of his feet.

"Later," the kid said. He hurried back to his friends, and the teens melted into the night.

So the neighborhood's top dog had arrived. Probably the local pusher, the man with power.

And Luke suffered another jolt. He wasn't much different from that pusher, either. All his life he'd been consumed by a need for power, respect.

And Amanda had understood that. She'd seen what drove him, and had challenged him to stop—to stop being that punk from Naked City, to stop trying to prove himself and let the past go.

To give up his plan for revenge.

Scowling at that thought, he climbed back into his car and started the engine. Harold Rothchild deserved to be taken down. He didn't have to question that goal. Rothchild had plenty of sins to account for in his life, including his mother's death.

But if Luke went through with his plan, if he evicted those people from their apartments, he'd be no better than Rothchild was. Or Amanda's ex-husband, for that matter—a man bent on revenge.

He'd lose Amanda's respect.

He'd lose her.

He was going to have to choose.

He gunned the Jaguar's engine, burning rubber as he screamed past the drug dealer's car. He sped to the corner, leaving Naked City behind in a cloud of exhaust.

But as he downshifted for an upcoming stop light, another insight jarred him. And he finally realized what had been plaguing him all night, the real source of his discontent. If he did what Amanda wanted and let go of the need for revenge, what would he have left?

It unnerved him that he didn't know.

"So you want to tell me what really happened the other night?" Kendall asked.

Amanda sat beside her sister on the steps in the

shallow end of the pool, water lapping over her hips. Sunshine sparkled off the rippling water. Birds chirped from the nearby hedge. Claire played on the tiles behind them, giggling and talking to her dolls.

And the last thing Amanda wanted to do was rehash her argument with Luke. She'd spent the past two days struggling to forget about it, trying to erase his words from her mind. But her thoughts kept veering back to that argument like a missile zeroing in on a target, replaying every word, every gesture, analyzing every awful second of that fight.

"Mandy?" Kendall pressed.

She sighed, knowing the futility of trying to elude her sister's questions. Kendall always wormed the truth out of her eventually, so she might as well confess all now. She pulled her knees to her chest, exhaled again. "Luke asked me to live with him, to stay here for a while."

Kendall's mouth dropped open. "Are you serious? Luke Montgomery asked you to move in with him?"

"Yes." She propped her chin on her knees. "I turned him down."

"He asked you to live here and you turned him down." Incredulity laced Kendall's voice.

"I didn't want to just live together. I wanted more." Her mouth twisted. "I wanted marriage, love, the whole deal."

"Oh, God. You're in love with him."

"Dumb, huh?" She managed a wobbly smile.

"No, you're not dumb. He's totally hot. But Luke Montgomery…" She shook her head.

"I know. Completely out of my league." And she only had herself to blame. Kendall had warned her. She'd known a billionaire would never fall in love with her. She'd known straight off that she wasn't his type.

"But he's not like you think he is," she added. "He's a good man, Kendall. Really good." Gentle, caring, protective. Lethal in a fight. Dominant in an extremely exciting way.

She shivered, remembering the hours of unending pleasure, the ecstasy she'd found in his arms. "I've never met anyone like him." And she knew she wouldn't again. Luke was unique. The man she loved. It had been the real deal for her.

Her chest aching, her eyes heavy with unshed tears, she watched a hawk soar silently overhead. And she struggled not to wonder what Luke was doing, what he was wearing, if he was thinking about her at all.

She scoffed at that thought. No doubt he was busy with his project—meeting with the investors, reviewing the plans, attending another glitzy party. He wasn't obsessing over their argument like she was. If he was, he would have called. She had to move on, forget it, stop torturing herself this way.

"Okay, let's break this down," Kendall said, pulling Amanda's attention back to her. "First off, he's obviously attracted to you. Even I could see that much."

"But that's not love."

Kendall pursed her lips, splashed water over her arms. "No, but he watches you. He's always aware of where you are. It's pretty intense, actually. Sexy."

Intense was right. She kept reliving those delirious sensations, his kiss, his touch, the way he'd driven her wild with desire. She'd spent hour after sleepless hour aching to be back in his arms.

"Sex isn't love, though. Not for a guy." She lowered her voice so Claire wouldn't hear. "And he wasn't proposing marriage. He was clear about that."

"That's still a pretty big thing, though, asking you to move in with him."

"Not big enough."

Her brow knitted, Kendall leaned back, propped herself on her elbows and stretched out her sculpted legs. "Are you sure it wasn't more? I mean, I know he's a billionaire and off the charts, but the way he looked at you…"

"I'm sure." The pressure on her chest increased. "And anyway, it's over now. We argued. He was furious."

"You argued about moving in?"

"Sort of." She blew out a heavy breath, turned her gaze to the palm fronds swishing overhead, the cloudless expanse of blue sky. "Mostly about our goals, though. He said I should go back to school, become an archaeologist like I wanted. He claimed I was too afraid to take a risk."

"He's right about that."

Amanda glared at her.

"Well, you are." Kendall's tone gentled. "Listen, you know I love you. And I'll take your side no matter what. But he's right. You've always been too cautious."

"And that's bad? If I hadn't been cautious and practical we would have starved."

"I know. And I owe you big-time for that. If you hadn't taken care of everything, held it all together… You even stayed with Mom after high school so I could dance. But that's the point. You need to do something fun for once. Something you want, just for yourself. You deserve it."

"But I can't just run off to school. Claire—"

"Claire will be fine. You know she will. And I'll help out. I'll do anything you want. I owe you that much after the way you took care of Mom."

"I don't know."

"Life's short, Mandy. You need to go for it before it's too late."

Amanda sighed, watched the sparkling water swirl past. Kendall made it sound easy. But she'd have to take courses, do fieldwork, get an advanced degree. It would take years. But she'd love to examine ancient artifacts, to explore caves like the one Luke owned. Excitement surged through her at the thought.

"Well, think about it." Kendall glanced at her watch. "Listen, I need to go. I don't want to miss rehearsal. But call me if you need me tonight."

Amanda rose with her and grabbed her towel. "No, I'm fine. I don't have anywhere to go now." Not since Luke's project had been approved. "If you could watch her tomorrow, though, that would be great. I need to move our stuff back to your house."

She didn't want to think about moving. It was the final step, the end of her hopes with Luke. But she couldn't put it off. "I'll drop her off early," she added. "Don't forget Luke's security people are coming by to install that system." And a bodyguard would arrive after that. Luke had made good on his promise to protect her, even if he didn't want her around.

She was still trying not to dwell on the thought of moving as she settled Claire down for a nap. She hadn't brought many things to Luke's house—some clothes, Claire's favorite toys, a few books—so she could move out in a couple of trips. At least she wouldn't prolong the agony. Still, just thinking of leaving made her want to weep.

"Mommy, nap with me," Claire pleaded as she tucked her in.

She perched on the edge of the bed, smoothed the hair from Claire's face. "I can't, honey. I need to finish filling out some papers and pack up our things."

Claire clutched her bear, whispered something against the fur.

"What?" Amanda bent down to hear.

"Bad man's coming. Brownie's scared."

Her heart tripped. Her daughter was afraid. "No one's going to hurt us. We're safe now. The bad man's in jail." At least, Wayne was. Candace Rothchild's killer still hadn't been caught.

She gnawed her lip, not wanting to think about that. But the bodyguard and security system would keep them safe.

"But I'll sit here with you for a while, okay?"

She rubbed Claire's back, tucked the blankets tighter around her, waiting for her to drift off. But Claire's anxiety bothered her—bothered her badly.

Ever since Claire had been born, she'd tried to keep her daughter safe, to give her the stable life she'd never had. She'd wanted Claire's childhood to be the opposite of hers—comforting, secure, with a mother she could depend on.

But she'd failed. First Wayne had threatened them, and then the danger had followed them here—terrible danger. And despite her precautions, Claire had sensed it. She'd picked up on the fear. And now she was turning into an anxious, insecure child, exactly what Amanda had hoped to avoid.

Claire's breathing deepened into sleep, and Amanda stood. Still nursing her injured ankle, she left the bedroom door ajar and walked back into the kitchen, her mind a jumble of thoughts. She couldn't blame herself for all their problems. The casino gunman had singled her out for some unknown reason. That certainly wasn't her fault.

She'd made a mistake with Wayne, though. She never should have married him.

She sank into the chair at the kitchen table, stared at the teaching application she still had to complete. She picked up her pen, then set it back down. She didn't feel like teaching again. But she did need a job.

She picked up the pen again, tapped it on the table, tried to drum up some enthusiasm. But it occurred to her that she'd been teaching Claire the wrong lesson. Maybe she shouldn't have emphasized safety all these years. Maybe she shouldn't have tried so hard to avoid risks.

Maybe she should have been teaching Claire to stop being afraid, to go after what she wanted in life and pursue her dreams.

She stared at the application, unable to avoid the truth. Luke was right. She was afraid to change. Change was scary, painful. It took courage and nerve. It was easier to cling to the known, to not risk failure, to find excuses not to try.

She'd asked him to change, though. She'd asked him to give up his lifelong goal, to abandon his need to avenge his mother's death.

And yet she wouldn't even change her career.

She'd been unfair.

Her forehead pounded; her stomach swirled with guilt. That argument *had* been about her. She was more mired in the past than he was.

She shoved the job application aside, pulled her laptop over and booted it up. She clicked on the University of Nevada Web site, searched their listing of graduate programs until she found the right one. Anthropology. She could study right here in Las Vegas. She could do everything she'd always dreamed.

If she was strong enough to try.

She sat back, her mind spinning with all she would have to do. She'd have to retake the Graduate Record Exam, submit an application. Money would be tight. She'd have to live with Kendall longer, find a babysitter for Claire.

But she could do this. She was stronger than she'd once thought. If she could face down Wayne, surely she could make this change. She reached for the teaching application and ripped it up.

She stood, headed for the wastepaper basket, her chest lighter now. Maybe this wouldn't solve all her problems, but it was a start.

But then the telephone rang. She stopped, swiveled to face it, her senses suddenly alert. The only person who had her number here was Luke.

Her pulse pounding, she crossed the room and answered the phone. "Hello?"

"Amanda." Luke's voice rumbled across the line, and she closed her eyes. And suddenly, all the emotion she'd been trying to hold at bay for the past two days broke loose, like a flash flood ravaging a desert gorge.

"Luke…" Her voice broke. Oh, God. Was he calling for another chance? Was he going to admit he was wrong?

"Can you stop by here tomorrow at noon to drop off the keys?" he asked.

"What?" She blinked, her emotions in turmoil, trying to recoup.

"The house keys. I'd like them back."

"Oh, right." She pressed her hand to her chest, struggled to breathe. He only wanted to finish this business, make sure she left on time and returned the keys. Their relationship was over. *Over.* She beat back the rising despair. "I'll be there."

"Good. My penthouse at noon." He cut the connection.

She sagged against the counter and closed her eyes. Tears clogged her throat. Anguish welled up inside, and she shuddered, consumed with regret. He didn't love her. He *really* didn't love her.

And she had to face the stark truth. She couldn't fantasize anymore, couldn't delude herself with false hopes. Her life would go on. She'd move back in with Kendall. She'd raise Claire and pursue her dreams.

But those dreams wouldn't include the man she loved.

Chapter 14

Her stomach jittering, Amanda clutched the handrail in Luke's private elevator as it rocketed to the forty-fifth floor. She trembled at the thought of seeing Luke again—for what could be the last time.

She'd barely slept all night, could hardly hold a thought in her mind. Her emotions careened from hope to dread, joy to despair like a dried leaf buffeted by a storm.

But she knew one thing. She had to maintain her dignity. She couldn't break down, couldn't embarrass Luke by making a scene. She'd simply drop off the keys, thank him for his help and then leave.

The elevator dinged and came to a stop, and the agitation in her belly grew. The door slid open, and she stepped out, her throat suddenly parched. Struggling for composure, she wiped her sweaty palms on her jeans, hoisted her battered purse over her shoulder, forced her feet to walk to his door.

She stopped, glanced back at the elevator, fought down the urge to bolt. This was ridiculous. She wasn't a coward. She could certainly hand him his keys. She inhaled and rapped on the door.

A second later he pulled it open, and her gaze shot to his. And for an eternity she couldn't breathe. She drank in his amber eyes, his somber brows, the sexy grooves framing his mouth. He'd shaved recently, and only the barest hint of whiskers darkened his jaw. Her gaze traveled over the wide ledge of his muscled shoulders, back to his sensual mouth.

And he stared back at her, his eyes roaming her face, her breasts. The hall turned stuffy and hot. Her lungs barely squeezed in air. She wanted desperately to hurl herself into his arms.

But he stepped back. "Come on in."

She nodded, pressed her lips together to suppress the words she shouldn't say. He led the way through the marbled entrance, past the elegant living room, to the windows at the opposite wall.

He turned then, and she abruptly stopped. She tightened her grip on her purse, suddenly tongue-tied, all thoughts wiped from her mind.

And he didn't make it easy for her. He just watched her, his expression unreadable, as if expecting her to speak.

The keys. Her face burned. "Oh, I, um…" She reached into her purse, fished around for the keys and pulled them out. "Here."

"Just set them on the table."

"Right." She placed them on the end table. Her gaze boomeranged back to his.

Seconds passed. She couldn't move. She could only stare at him, soaking in the sight of his face while emotions tumbled inside her—there was so much she wanted to say.

But he didn't want to hear her explanations. If he'd changed his mind about their relationship, he would have told her by now. Instead, he'd only phoned once in the past two days to tell her to drop off the keys.

"You want something to drink?" he asked.

She should refuse. He was being polite. He had work to do, people to see. He might even have a date.

That thought made her want to wretch. She pressed her hand to her belly to quiet her nerves. "No thanks, I—"

"A glass of wine." He strode to the mahogany sideboard, and she struggled to compose herself.

"All right." One glass. She could handle that.

His back muscles flexed as he pulled out a bottle. He worked the corkscrew, extracted the cork with a muffled pop. Her gaze traced the riveting bulge of his biceps, the tendons that ran down his strong arms.

And she wondered how many women had pined for him, how many hearts he'd broken over the years. Wasn't that what they'd said about Candace Rothchild—that she'd been obsessed with Luke? He'd even had a restraining order issued in an attempt to keep her away.

Amanda could hardly blame her. She'd certainly never forget this man. Too choked up to speak, she dragged her gaze to the window and stared unseeing at the city below.

"Here you go." His breath brushed her ear, and she jumped. She hadn't even seen him approach. She inhaled his arousing scent, took the wine glass with quivering hands. She wanted to touch him so badly that she had to take a step back.

She sipped her wine. The silence stretched. He stared at her, his dark brows knitted together, and she had no idea what to say.

And she realized she'd made a mistake. She never should have come here and tortured herself this way. Kendall could have dropped off the keys.

"How's Claire?" he suddenly asked.

"Good. Great." She gulped her wine, and he fell silent again.

"Thank you for letting us stay at your house," she added. "And for what you did with Wayne… For everything."

Oh, God. She was dying here. Why didn't he say anything? She needed to end this ordeal before she completely broke down.

He frowned, looking uncertain suddenly, and a fierce pang of longing lanced her heart. What she wouldn't give to run her hands down his back, feel his muscles flex under her palms. Feel his raw urgency fueling hers.

"More wine?" he asked. She jerked her gaze to her glass, realized with a start that she'd drained it without even being aware.

"No. No, thanks." Breathless, she set the glass on the table next to the keys. How pathetic could she get? She was standing here fantasizing about him, ogling him, her desire clear in her eyes, while he waited for her to leave.

"Well, I'd better go." Before she broke down and begged.

"Amanda." His eyes met hers. He shoved his hand through his hair. "About the project—"

"It was none of my business, really." She twisted her hands, and the words broke loose. "I'm sorry. I shouldn't have said anything. It wasn't my place. Just forget it, okay? And you were right. About me, I mean. I—"

"Amanda—"

"I'm not going to teach. I threw the application away. I'm going to go back to school."

"You are?"

She nodded, her face flaming. So much for dignity and restraint.

The doorbell buzzed. Luke glanced at the door, then back at her.

"Anyhow," she added. "There's your key…and I need to go now. You're busy, and I—"

"No. Wait." He held up a hand. "Stay there. I have something to say."

He strode to the door, and she crossed her arms, wishing again that she'd never come. Luke didn't want to hear her news.

She glanced around the penthouse knowing it would be for the final time. Her gaze landed on the desk where they'd made love, and the images came tumbling back before she could stop them—Luke's eyes glittering with hunger, his mouth hot against hers. That electrifying way he'd watched her, his stark need driving him hard.

She swallowed, her breathing suddenly ragged. She looked at Luke at the door. This wasn't going to work. She had to get out of here now.

She headed toward him just as he shut the door and turned back. He glanced at the envelope in his hand, tore it open, pulled out the letter inside. His frown deepened, and he grew suddenly still.

Something was wrong. "What is it?"

His gaze rose to hers. The fierce intensity of his expression made her breath halt.

"It's another note, like the one you got."

Shock billowed through her. She pressed her hand to her throat. "You mean from the killer?"

"Yeah. He says to meet him in the blackjack pit."

"Now? He's here? In the casino?"

"So it seems." He crossed to the phone, picked up the receiver, then swore. "The line's dead."

"Dead?" Her blood drained from her face. How had he cut the phone lines? Any why? What did that killer have planned?

Luke tossed the note onto the table, tugged his cell phone from the pocket of his slacks. He punched in a number, waited, and his eyes turned even grimmer. "The lines must all be down. No one's picking up in security."

He tapped in another number, waited, then shook his head. "Voice mail. Something big must be happening if Matt's not answering his phone."

She bit her lip. "What are you going to do?"

"Alert security." He snapped his phone closed, slipped it into his pocket again. "Stay here. I'll be right back. You have your cell phone?"

"Yes, but—"

"Good. Call me if anything happens. And whatever you do, don't leave."

"I won't." She watched him head for the door. But that killer would be armed. "Luke," she said, her fear for him making her voice shake. "Be careful."

He paused, turned back, and his eyes held hers. "I will." And for several heartbeats, he just gazed at her, and beyond the urgency, beyond the determination, lay something deeper, something more intimate. Something that looked a lot like love.

"When I get back, we're going to talk," he promised, his voice gruff. "Now lock the door and stay put." He pivoted and strode out the door.

The door clicked shut. She raced to lock it, then sagged against the wall. Had that really been love she'd seen in his eyes? Was it possible that they'd have another chance?

She couldn't get up her hopes. She could be imagining things. Because if he loved her, then why hadn't he called? And why make her return the house keys? He was even having a security system installed in Kendall's house—a clear sign he wanted her gone.

But she couldn't think about that now, not with the killer so close. She had to stay calm, stay alert. Luke might call for her help.

She dug in her purse for her cell phone, then saw that the battery was dead. She hissed out her breath. Now what was she going to do?

Calm down, she decided. Becoming hysterical wouldn't do Luke any good. She'd just sit tight and wait for him to return.

The doorbell buzzed. Her heart jerked into her throat. She whipped around and faced the door.

Was that security? The killer? Luke couldn't be returning so soon.

She pressed her hand to her rioting chest, willing her pulse to slow. She was acting paranoid. It was probably just Luke. She couldn't let her imagination run wild.

"Who is it?" she called.

No one answered.

Her heart raced even more.

She eyed the phone—no help there. Her gaze landed on the hutch nearby and she saw the room key. He must have forgotten it. And now he'd come back to get it.

But then why didn't he answer? And returning for his room key hardly seemed like a priority with a killer running loose.

Unless he needed it to gain access to private areas of the hotel.

"Luke?" Her nerves twisting even tighter, she pressed her ear to the door. Silence. "Who's there?" she called again.

Nothing. Maybe he couldn't hear her through the door.

Her hands trembling, she scooped up the room key. But then she hesitated again. She couldn't open the door without knowing who was there. What if it wasn't Luke?

The door lock clicked. She watched in horror as the handle began to dip. Someone was coming inside.

And Luke didn't have his key.

Her heart raced wildly. She had to run, escape. *Move.*

She whipped around, searching frantically for a place to hide. She raced down Luke's hallway, ducked behind his bedroom door. She heard the door to the penthouse open and bang against the wall.

She stayed as still as she could and hugged her arms, struggling not to make any noise. It could be the killer. She couldn't let him know she was back here. But he already knew that. Like an idiot, she'd called out, giving herself away.

She listened hard, but her blood pressure roared in her ears. Terrified, needing to find out where he was, she inched back to the edge of the door.

She peeked out. A waiter stood in the entrance next to a room service cart.

Room service. She frowned, suddenly confused.

Maybe she'd overreacted. Maybe Luke had ordered lunch before she'd arrived. But then the waiter turned toward her, and she spotted the gun.

For a second, she stood petrified. The intruder's cold gaze slammed into hers. Then she gasped, jerked back behind the door.

It was the man from the Rothchild's casino, the same man who'd drugged her. And he'd just seen her. She had to run.

But where?

Frantic, she tried to think. The balcony was out. She was forty-five floors up. And all the phone lines were dead.

She dithered, then rushed through Luke's bedroom, raw terror fueling her steps. She should have gone into the kitchen. Back here there was only the bathroom—no way out.

A bullet whined past, splintering the wall beside her head, and the sharp bang deafened her ears. She shrieked, dove into the bathroom, searching for a way to defend herself.

But there was nothing. Not even a can of shaving cream. Her entire body shook.

And then she smelled it. That aftershave. The stench slithered through the air and assaulted her nose.

Her knees quivered hard. She turned and met the killer's eyes.

"All right," he said, and the sound of his voice made her heart quake. "I want that ring. And I want it now."

What the hell was happening? Why hadn't the gunman shown up?

Scowling, Luke hurried back through the hallway

from the security office, his apprehension mounting with each long stride. No one had reported any problems. The phones were still out, but the telephone company had it in hand. He'd alerted the police, posted guards throughout the casino, sent another to check on Amanda while he waited in the blackjack pit for the killer to show.

No one had come.

But why send a note and not show up?

Unless the killer had lost his nerve. Or the extra security guards had scared him off.

But then why did this fear keep gnawing at him, the feeling that something was wrong? The feeling that he'd missed something—something urgent. That danger lurked close.

And why didn't Matt Schaffer answer his cell phone? No one knew where he'd gone—which was too damned strange. His security chief never took time off on the job.

He reached the service elevators, spotted the housekeeping manager checking a maid's cleaning cart. "Has anyone gone up to my suite?" he asked.

She shook her head. "No, sir. Would you like something sent up?"

"No. So no one's used the elevator?"

She frowned. "No one from housekeeping."

"Room service just went up," the young maid beside her said. "He said he had your lunch."

Room service? He hadn't ordered food.

Dread slithered into his gut.

Amanda was there. He'd left her in his penthouse. *Alone.* Swearing, he ran to the elevator, swiped his spare key card in, then punched in the access code.

What had he been thinking? What if the security

guard had arrived too late? The gunman had been after her from the start.

And that note had been nothing but a decoy, a ploy to get her alone.

The elevator started up.

And Luke began to sweat.

Amanda stared down the barrel of the pistol. She was trapped in her worst nightmare, facing a killer. And now she was going to die.

This man had murdered Candace Rothchild. He'd bludgeoned the woman to death. And now he was going to kill her, too. She could see it in his cold, dead eyes.

Terror fought its way up her throat, building, swelling, threatening to explode in a primal shriek. She choked it back, wheezed a breath past her paralyzed lungs. She had to stay in control.

"Give me the ring," he repeated, his fury clear in his voice.

"I don't have it," she said, hating how badly her voice shook. "I told you that the other night."

His eyes hardened. The stench of his aftershave reeked in the air. "You have it. It's in your purse. Hand it over now."

In her purse? Her lips quivered, and she shook her head. "You're wrong. You have me confused with someone else. I don't have it. Really I don't."

"Like hell you don't. I put it there. In the lobby," he added at her blank look. "When your purse spilled on the floor."

She gaped at him. That had been planned? He'd bumped her, planted the ring in her purse. But then he'd changed clothes, accosted her with the gun. But why? It didn't make any sense.

She jerked her purse off her shoulder, held it out. "Here. Take it. Look for yourself." And as soon as he was distracted, she'd bolt past him out the door.

But he was too smart. He shook his head. "Dump it out. Right there."

Her throat convulsed. She wasn't going to get away. Her hands trembling, she pulled open the purse's draw-string, then inverted the contents onto the floor. Tissues tumbled out, then her nail clippers, her car keys, a couple of pens. She shook the bag, and her wallet followed, along with a comb and a travel-sized mirror.

"That's it," she whispered, her eyes on his. She flapped the bag again, but nothing else came out. "I told you, it isn't here."

"It has to be." His face turned red, his voice vibrating with rage.

And images flashed before her eyes—Claire holding her bear…her tiny arms reaching for a hug…Claire's sweet, flushed face as she slept. Luke risking his life to protect her…the hunger burning in his sexy eyes…the incredible bliss he brought to her life.

And suddenly she snapped. She didn't deserve this fear. She didn't deserve to die. And she was fed up with being the victim, fed up with being pushed around and attacked.

Wayne had been bad enough. She'd made a mistake, suffered a lapse in judgment and had paid the price.

But this creep—who the hell was he to threaten her?

"I don't have your ring," she gritted out, walking toward him. She gripped the straps of her empty purse. "I told you that from the start. Now leave me alone."

Furious, she whipped the purse forward, slapping the leather across his face.

The gun fired.

Heat tore through her shoulder, and she screamed.

Chapter 15

Amanda had been shot. *Shot.*

Her scream still echoing in his skull, Luke glanced around the hallway outside his penthouse, took in the dead guard slumped by the door. He slammed his key card into the lock, kicked the door open, and it crashed back against the wall.

He burst inside, desperate to find her, then frantically scanned the room. Empty. *Damn.* Where had that bastard taken her?

A soft cry drifted from down the hall.

Adrenaline stormed through his veins, but he fought to contain it, knowing he'd endanger her if he rushed. Forcing himself to walk softly—to not alert the gunman—he inched his way down the hall.

He'd never forgive himself if Amanda died. He'd been a fool to leave her alone. He pushed the panic to the back of his mind, refusing to think about that now. He had to focus, concentrate to keep her alive.

When he reached his bedroom door, he paused. He listened intently, but silence thundered back. Where the hell had they gone?

He flattened himself against the wall, then peeked inside. Nothing. The bedroom was empty. Only the bathroom was left.

He raced across the bedroom, pressed himself to the wall by the bathroom door, and listened again. And then suddenly he heard Amanda. She let out an agonized moan.

She was injured. She had to be bleeding. He felt wild at the thought. He clenched his hands into fists, trying not to let his mind go there…trying not to think about her suffering, dying.

He loved her.

The realization bolted out of nowhere, but he instantly knew it was true. He loved her. Amanda was his destiny. And he wasn't going to let her die.

His mind shut down. His vision hazed. The primitive need to avenge her raged.

And he couldn't control it anymore. He burst through the doorway into the bathroom. In a glance, he took in Amanda lying in a pool of blood, the gunman kneeling a short distance away.

Crazed now, insane with the need to protect her, Luke flew at the killer with a guttural cry. He slammed into his side, flattened him to the marble floor. And then he rammed his fist into his face, grunting, pounding, hitting him again and again, punching his jaw, his gut, his head.

The gunman stopped struggling and went slack.

"Luke," Amanda called. "Luke, stop." Her weak voice penetrated the haze.

He sat back on his heels, hauled in air to his heaving lungs, studied the unconscious man sprawled on the floor—the same man who'd attacked them in the hills. He confiscated the gun, whipped out his cell phone and called 911, then rushed to Amanda's side.

Oh, hell. Her face was too white. Blood seeped from her shoulder onto the tiles. Alarmed, he leaped up and grabbed a towel, then pressed it to her shoulder to staunch the flow. "Hold on," he urged her.

She peered up at him. Her pale lips tightened with pain. "Luke," she whispered.

"I love you," he told her, and pressed the wadded towel down hard.

She whimpered. Her eyes rolled back, and she went slack.

Frantic, terrified that she would die, he felt her wrist and checked her pulse. It was weak, but she was alive. He sagged back on his heels in relief.

But then he leaned toward her again, cradling her as best he could, keeping the towel pressed over her wound. She was so pale, so blasted weak. His throat wedged tight with dread. And he just held her, soothing her—this amazing woman he loved.

An eternity later, voices shouted down the hall. And then people swirled around him, police, paramedics. Radios squawked. Gurneys rolled in. People barked out orders and unloaded supplies. In his peripheral vision, he saw the police handcuff the gunman and haul him away.

"Mr. Montgomery," someone said. Luke ignored him, his entire attention focused on Amanda's face, willing her to survive. Her lips were tinged blue, her face so pale that her freckles stood out on her nose.

"Mr. Montgomery, you'll have to let go so we can help her. Please let go, sir. She needs our help."

The paramedics. "Right." He had to let her go.

The hell he did. He pried his hand from the towel, forced himself to rise and step back. The paramedics swarmed her, checking her vital signs, giving her oxygen, strapping her pale, fragile body into a gurney and rushing away.

And he knew right then that he couldn't do it. No matter what else happened in his life, no matter what anyone wanted, he could never let this woman go.

He loved her. And she was forever his.

Amanda surfaced from a deep, dark haze hours later. She blinked her eyes open, then zeroed in on Luke. He sat slumped in an armchair across the hospital room, his gaze trained on her.

He instantly leaped to his feet. "You're awake."

He rushed to her side, perched on the edge of her cot, and she couldn't take her eyes from his face. His hair wasn't combed. Black bristles coated his jaw. And he looked so dear, so much like everything she'd ever wanted, that tears sprang to her eyes.

He grabbed a glass from the metal table beside the cot. "Your throat's raw from the surgery. You've been out for a couple of hours."

He adjusted the straw, brought the glass to her face and she took a cooling sip. Her right hand was hooked to an IV. Heavy bandages encased her left shoulder, making it impossible to move. She thought back, tried to sort through the morass of memories—the gunman's chilling eyes, his rage when he didn't find the ring, the huge satisfaction she'd felt at whipping his face with her purse. Then excruciating pain. Luke bursting in.

Had he really told her he loved her?

Or had she hallucinated that part?

"They removed the bullet from your shoulder," he told her, not budging from the bed. She closed her eyes, enjoying the warm, solid feel of him, the way his thigh wedged securely against her hip.

"The doctor said it all went well," he added. He picked up her left hand and stroked it, and she sighed at how comforting that felt. "No complications. The bullet missed the critical parts. He's stopping by later to explain the operation and rehab."

"Gunman," she said around the dryness in her throat.

Luke helped her take another sip of water and made a sound of disgust. "The guy's a Houdini. He escaped. It was the damnedest thing. They had him handcuffed and were waiting downstairs for another ambulance to arrive. Somehow he got out of the cuffs, overpowered another guard and used his clothes as a disguise. No one knows how he did it. But he's smart. He even knocked out Matt Schaffer earlier to steal his key."

Her heart dove. So the killer was on the loose again. The danger wasn't gone.

"Don't worry," he added, as if reading her mind. "I've hired more bodyguards for you and Claire. And I've added even more security to my house. Claire's coming by later, by the way. Kendall thought it was better to wait."

Amanda frowned, wondering if the painkillers had muddled her mind. Why was he talking about his house?

He leaned closer, and his face was inches from hers.

She traced the crinkles at the corner of his eyes with her gaze, the faint lines creasing his brow. But his somber expression made her heart lurch.

"I'm sorry, Amanda. I never should have left you alone."

"Not your fault," she rasped out.

"Yeah, it was. It was my fault you were even there. If it hadn't been for the plans I wanted to show you... And then when I heard you scream...

"It almost killed me," he confessed, his voice so anguished it brought a lump to her throat. "Seeing you bleeding on the floor..."

He shook his head, and his voice turned fierce. "I won't make that mistake again. I'm keeping you safe for the rest of your life."

Her heart beat fast. She stared at him, not sure she understood.

"I know this isn't romantic," he said. "You deserve better. And I'll ask you again later, somewhere with flowers, music..." He shoved his hand through his hair. "Hell, I don't even have the ring. I left it in my safe. But I can't wait. I need to know."

His eyes pleaded with hers. "I love you, Amanda. Marry me."

Her lips parted in shock. He loved her? She hadn't imagined that part? "You bought me a ring?"

"I was miserable without you. You were right about the project, about the revenge. I didn't call you because I was having the plans redrawn. That's what I've been doing for the past two days, overseeing the drawings. I wanted to wait until they were done."

Her breath hitched. "You changed the project?"

"You'll like it." He traced the veins on her hand with

his thumb, sending shivers racing over her skin. "The investors are happy. It's still basically the same, but we modified it so it's more like a village. There's a training center attached, a place for career counseling, some affordable housing, too."

She squeezed his hand, her heart filled with love for this man. "It sounds perfect. You're perfect. I love you, Luke."

He reached out and touched her cheek. He gazed at her with so much love in his eyes that her own eyes flooded with tears. "Then you'll marry me?" he asked.

"I'll marry you. As long as you don't mind being married to a student. I'm going to be in school for the next few years."

His lips curved up. A sexy gleam lit his eyes. "I've got a cave you could survey—for the right price."

She smiled back. "A price, hmm? And just how much will this cave cost?"

His eyes heated. "You. Every day for the rest of my life."

"It's a deal," she whispered. And then his mouth captured hers, and she didn't speak again for a long, long while.

Two weeks later, Amanda put on her final touch of lipstick, then appraised herself in the bathroom mirror. Her skin color had rebounded since the shooting. Her dark circles had faded, thanks to Luke's constant pampering and insistence that she rest.

This was her first night out without the shoulder harness, and she was making the most of it with her slinky red dress—the same one she'd worn the night she met Luke.

Of course, she wore a few new accessories with the

outfit now—a brilliant gold choker necklace and matching earrings. A fabulous antique diamond engagement ring. She stretched out her fingers and smiled at the gorgeous stone.

"Ring, Mommy," Claire called from the other room.

"Just give me a minute." Her lips curved in amusement. Claire loved to look at her ring and admire how the diamond caught the light. Luke joked that they had a future gemologist in their midst.

"My ring," Claire said again.

Amanda misted herself with a bold new scent, then dragged in her breath. That was the best she could do. She just hoped it was good enough to catch Luke's attention tonight. Now that her shoulder was mending, she had a list of very sensual demands she was going to insist he fulfill.

She turned off the bathroom light, walked into her bedroom. Claire sat in the middle of the bed, surrounded by the contents of her purse.

"Oh, Claire. I have to leave soon, and I need my purse." She slipped on her high heels, then crossed to the bed. "Let's put everything back, okay?"

"My ring, Mommy." Claire held up her fist, and Amanda frowned.

"What have you got there?"

"My ring." Claire opened her small hand, and Amanda's jaw dropped. An enormous diamond ring sat in her palm.

She propped her hip on the bed, so stunned she could hardly breathe. "Let me see." Claire handed it over, and she held it up to the light.

"Oh, my God." It was incredible. Six or seven carats minimum, the diamond unlike anything she'd ever seen.

At least she thought it was a diamond. Colors sparkled and swirled in the center of the stone, changing from blue to violet to green.

"What are you doing?" Luke asked from the doorway.

She couldn't take her eyes off the stone. "Luke, look at this. You won't believe it." She held up the ring, and he frowned.

He strode to the bed and she rose, handing it to him. He studied it for a second, then let out a long, admiring whistle. "Well, I'll be damned. It's the missing ring. The Tears of the Quetzal. The one Candace Rothchild had."

"But where did it come from?" She jerked her gaze to Claire. "Where on earth did you find this?"

"Your purse," Claire said, and her bottom lip trembled. "My ring."

Amanda picked up her purse, staring at it in disbelief. "But it wasn't in here. I know it wasn't. I dumped everything out."

"In the hole, Mommy."

"The hole?"

She opened the empty bag and checked inside. She pulled the lining up, and sure enough, a hole had ripped along the seam, fraying the silky fabric. Her gaze flew to Luke's. "She's right. There is a hole. The ring must have worked its way through. It's been there all along."

His forehead furrowed. "We'd better get it to the police right away. We can drop it off on our way out."

"Good idea."

"We can't keep this ring," Luke said to Claire, his voice gentle. "Someone lost it, and we need to take it back. But how about if we buy you a special ring tomorrow? Will that be all right?"

"You could ask Aunt Kendall if she'd like to shop with us," Amanda added, and Claire consulted her bear.

"Okay. Aunt Kendall," Claire called, and scrambled off the bed. She raced from the bedroom, and Amanda smiled.

"I still can't believe we found the ring. It's gorgeous."

"Yeah, gorgeous." His gaze burned into hers, then dipped lazily over her lips, her throat...her breasts.

"They say it has a legend," she said, suddenly breathless. "That whoever has it falls instantly in love."

He moved closer, and his eyes turned hotter yet. "You think the legend came true?" His voice came out graveled and deep.

Her heart pounded fast. And she remembered the first time she'd seen him, right after her purse had spilled, just seconds after that gunman had slipped the ring inside. She'd definitely found true love at first sight.

"So what do you think?" he repeated, moving closer. And then his hands were on her back, her hips, pulling her firmly against him. Her body softened, anticipating his touch, and she dropped her head back with a sigh.

"Is the legend true?" he asked again.

"I think," she whispered back, "that at the rate we're going, we're worthy of a legend of our own."

He grunted in agreement. And then his mouth took hers, and she showed him her deep abiding love.

Epilogue

The man hunched behind the wheel of his car under the cover of darkness. He waited, his gut seething, his gaze trained on the police station door.

Damn them all. Damn the woman for hiding the ring. Damn Luke Montgomery for holing her up in his house. And damn the Las Vegas traffic that had kept him from overtaking Montgomery's car tonight. He'd been watching their house for the past two weeks, waiting for a chance at that ring.

But Montgomery had foiled him—again. He fingered the bruise discoloring his jaw, the ribs still aching from Montgomery's fists. He'd underestimated that billionaire.

His mistake.

The police station doors swung open just then. Montgomery and his woman strolled out, then paused in a circle of light. Montgomery pulled her close, and they started kissing, getting so hot and heavy he nearly blew the horn to force them apart. But they finally stopped and strolled away.

So the police had the ring now. It didn't matter. This was a blip, just a minor bump in the road. He'd lost the ring, but he would recoup. He would change his strategy, turn this to his advantage, let this lull them into thinking the matter was done.

And then he would strike.

One by one, he'd vowed. He let out a high-pitched laugh. If anyone thought this was over, they were dead wrong.

* * * * *

In honor of our 60th anniversary,
Harlequin® American Romance® is celebrating
by featuring an all-American male each month,
all year long with
MEN MADE IN AMERICA!
This June, we'll be featuring American men
living in the West.

Here's a sneak preview of
THE CHIEF RANGER by Rebecca Winters.

Chief Ranger Vance Rossiter has to confront the
sister of a man who died while under Vance's
watch...and also confront his attraction to her.

"Chief Ranger Rossiter?" The sight of the woman who'd stepped inside Vance's office brought him to his feet. "I'm Rachel Darrow. Your secretary said I should come right in."

"Please," he said, walking around his desk to shake her hand. At a glance he estimated she was in her mid-twenties. Her feminine curves did wonders for the pale blue T-shirt and jeans she was wearing. "Ranger Jarvis informed me there's a young boy with you."

The unfriendly expression in her beautiful green eyes caught him off guard. "Yes," was her clipped reply. "When we arrived in Yosemite the ranger told me I couldn't go anywhere in the park until I talked to you first."

"That's right."

"Knowing you wanted this meeting to be private, he offered to show my nephew around Headquarters."

So this woman was the victim's sister… "What's his name?"

"Nicky."

The boy who haunted Vance's dreams now had a name. "How old is he?"

"He turned six three weeks ago. Were you the man in charge when my brother and sister-in-law were killed?"

"Yes. To tell you I'm sorry for what happened couldn't begin to convey my feelings."

The woman's gaze didn't flicker. "I won't even try to describe mine. Just tell me one thing. Was their accident preventable?"

"Yes," he answered without hesitation.

"In other words, the people working under you fell asleep on your watch and two lives were snuffed out as a result."

Hearing it put like that, he had to set the record straight. "My staff had nothing to do with it. I, myself, could have prevented the loss of life."

Ms. Darrow's expression hardened. "So you admit culpability."

"Yes. I take full blame."

A look of pain crossed over her features. "You can just stand there and admit it?" Her cry echoed that of his own tortured soul.

"Yes." He sucked in his breath.

"I work for a cruise line. Aboard ship, it's the captain's responsibility to maintain rigid safety regulations. If a disaster like that had happened while he was in charge he would have been relieved of his command and never given another ship again."

Rachel Darrow couldn't know she was preaching to the converted. "If you've come to the park with the intention of bringing a lawsuit against me for negligence, maybe you should." It would only be what he deserved.

"Maybe I will."

In the next instant, she wheeled around and hurried out of his office. Vance could have gone after her, but it would cause a scene, something he was loath to do for a variety of reasons. In the first place, he needed to cool down before he approached her again.

The discovery of the Darrows' frozen bodies had affected every ranger in the park. A little boy had been orphaned—a boy whose aunt was all he had left.

* * * * *

Will Rachel allow Vance to explain—
and will she let him into her heart?
Find out in
THE CHIEF RANGER
Available June 2009 from
Harlequin® American Romance®.

We'll be spotlighting a different series every month
throughout 2009 to celebrate our 60th anniversary.

Look for Harlequin®
American Romance® in June!

Join us for a year-long celebration of the rugged
American male! From cops to cowboys—
Men Made in America has the hero
you've been dreaming about!

Look for

The Chief Ranger

by Rebecca Winters, on sale in June!

REQUEST YOUR FREE BOOKS!

2 FREE NOVELS PLUS 2 FREE GIFTS!

Silhouette® Romantic SUSPENSE

Sparked by Danger, Fueled by Passion!